Fate That Twists Her

APPLEMAN'S GAP
BOOK THREE

KELLY UTT

2024 Standards of Starlight Paperback Edition

www.standardsofstarlight.com

Cover art by Elizabeth Mackey

ISBN: 978-1-952893-33-9

A Note on Setting

While many of the locations in this book are true to life, some details of the setting have been changed.

Appleman's Gap is a fictional town, set about an hour east of Nashville, Tennessee on the edge of the Cumberland Plateau. I envision it much like the mountainous region of the Appalachians in East Tennessee, but placed closer to Nashville. It's a small town along a winding river that empties into a picturesque lake with a bustling marina. Apple orchards line the hillsides and a railroad skirts the river bank.

Nashville, of course, is a real town, the bustling, creative capital of the U.S. state of Tennessee. Our characters in the Appleman's Gap series often go to Nashville since the fictional town is considered to be within the Nashville metro area. Like the real-life Nashville metro area, Appleman's Gap is experiencing rapid growth with new residents moving in and new construction happening everywhere.

Fate That Twists Her is a work of fiction. Any references to historical events, real people, or real places are used fictitiously. Other names, characters, places, and events are products of my imagination, and any resemblance to actual events or places or persons, living or dead, is entirely coincidental.

Thanks for reading,
Kelly Utt

PART ONE

Time to Move

One

LAUREL DANE RECLINED on her plush gray sofa, the only piece of furniture in her Washington, D.C-area condo that hadn't yet been loaded onto the moving truck. Her burgeoning belly was becoming unwieldy. She wouldn't have been much help, if she'd tried.

"I'm supervising," she said playfully as Brad walked past with his umpteenth box of household goods.

Brad chuckled, adjusting his grip on the box. "Supervising? Is that what we're calling it now?" He bent over to kiss her gently on the lips.

Laurel grinned, patting her belly. "That's right. Baby and I are doing the hard work here."

Mikey, Maggie, Hazel, and Ryan bustled around, each sibling carrying boxes and carefully wrapping fragile items. The camaraderie and banter between them filled the space with warmth and laughter. It had been a long time since the five of them were all together outside of an event hosted by their parents. There was a different energy within the group today. It was nice.

Ryan, the youngest of the Dane siblings, approached with a lopsided smile. "Need anything, Sis?"

Ryan had been generous in not holding it against Laurel that she'd suspected him of fathering Jamie Beck's baby. He was a decent guy. Especially because he'd also expressed support for their dad, who was the actual father of the young woman's love child. Ryan's wavy, dark hair contrasted with the blues in his flannel shirt. He looked like he was ready to star in some teeny-bopper clothing company's ad. That or a boy band, should those ever make a comeback.

Laurel shook her head. "Just keep doing what you're doing. You all are amazing."

Hazel rolled her eyes as she walked by with a stack of books. "Don't let it go to your head. We're only doing this because you're pregnant."

Hazel was probably irritable because she'd left her cats, Crook and Chase, at home with their mom. That and the fact that Laurel had played a part in Hazel's boyfriend being arrested a few months back. Hazel had liked Kevin Clark, despite his involvement with the criminal element in their hometown.

Hazel's hair was nearly the same shade of dark brown as Ryan's, making the two youngest Dane siblings look so similar, they could pass as twins. Fraternal twins, of course, but people rarely thought about specifics like that. Hazel and Ryan appeared to go together. The family resemblance was strong.

"Yeah, right," Maggie chimed in, placing a box of kitchenware on the floor. "We all know you're the favorite. We're just living up to our reputations as the dutiful siblings."

Laurel laughed. "And you're doing a fantastic job of it."

The sound of tape being pulled and boxes being shuffled filled the air. Despite the chaos of moving, there was a sense of camaraderie that Laurel cherished. They were a team, a family, and soon they'd all be back in Appleman's Gap, facing whatever challenges awaited them.

It had taken Laurel a long time and a lot of soul searching to make the decision to move back to Tennessee. The Washington, D.C. area—and specifically, her condo in Arlington—had been her happy home for years. She had been recruited by the F.B.I. in D.C. while playing French horn for the U.S. Navy Band, and she'd started her law-enforcement career there after completing training in Quantico. Laurel and Brad had met and fallen in love in the D.C. area. His condo had been just a few miles away in Alexandria, before he'd sold it and moved to Appleman's Gap. The bottom line—she had become a full-fledged adult in our nation's capital. The city would always hold a special place in her heart.

Brad appeared again, slightly out of breath. His muscles rippled. Laurel wasn't sure whether he was flexing on purpose, but she enjoyed the show.

"The truck's almost full. Just a few more boxes to go," he said. "And that sofa."

"Good," Laurel said. "I'm ready for a break."

The door to the condo swung open, and Jimmy Paulson walked in, looking around at the half-empty space. Laurel's friend and Special Agent in Charge was still noticeably tanned from his trip to Antigua a couple of months prior. You could tell because he was bald as a q-ball. The top of his head was a darker shade than his usual light pink. Laurel put a hand over her mouth, amused.

"Looks like you guys have been busy," Jimmy said.

"Just a bit," Brad replied, wiping sweat from his forehead. It was late March, and temps outside were beginning to warm. "Glad you could make it."

Jimmy grinned. "Wouldn't miss it. Where do you need me?"

"Anywhere you see a box," Laurel said, pointing toward the kitchen.

"You're gonna sit around and watch us work?" he asked her, teasingly.

"That's the plan."

Jimmy joined in the effort, quickly blending into the rhythm of packing and moving. Despite his tough exterior and gruff demeanor, he was a natural fit with the Dane siblings. Laurel appreciated his presence, knowing he had come to mean a lot to her over the past few years.

After the last box was loaded onto the truck, they all stood around the condo, surveying the now-empty space. It felt surreal to Laurel, leaving behind the life she had built in D.C. for the uncertainty that awaited back home.

"All right, troops," Brad announced, clapping his hands together. "Let's head to the Cherry Blossom Festival for some fun before we hit the road tomorrow morning. The blooms are one of the most spectacular things you'll ever see."

Laurel nodded. "Yeah, it wouldn't be right to visit when the festival is happening and not go see all of that beauty in person. They're crowning the Cherry Blossom Queen this afternoon at the Capitol Hilton."

"Don't forget the parade," Jimmy added. "It's happening first."

The group agreed enthusiastically, eager for a bit of fun after the morning's hard work. The Danes and Brad would all be staying in a hotel that evening, since there were no beds left in Laurel's condo. It was beginning to feel like they were all on vacation together.

With Brad's arm wrapped snugly around her waist, Laurel said a tearful goodbye to her former home. Then they piled onto the Metrorail and headed to the spot on Constitution Avenue where they'd watch the procession.

As they made their way to the festival, the city was alive with the sights and sounds of spring. The cherry blossoms were in full bloom, painting the landscape with delicate pinks and whites. The festival atmosphere was infectious, lifting everyone's spirits. Even the aroma filling the air was sweet from the fragrant blooms. It reminded Laurel of the scent of the Dane family's apple orchard in spring. It made her smile.

The group arrived downtown, joining the throngs of people enjoying the festivities. Food vendors, performers, and artists filled the area, creating a vibrant tapestry of activity. They found a spot near the edge of the street where they could watch the colorful floats and marching bands go by.

"Look at that one!" Hazel exclaimed, pointing to a float adorned with cherry blossom trees and traditional Japanese lanterns. "It's beautiful."

Mikey nodded in agreement. "It sure is. Makes you appreciate the effort people put into these things. I'll bet most of these floats took hours to make."

"More like days," Brad said.

"True, true," Ryan agreed.

When the parade was finished, Laurel, Brad, and the siblings strolled through the festival, enjoying the sights and sounds as they moved toward the Hilton. They paused at various booths, sampling treats and admiring the crafts on display. It was a perfect way to unwind after the hectic morning.

"Look over there," Hazel said, pointing towards the main stage set up outside of the hotel. She was becoming more relaxed, thanks to a couple of beers she'd purchased from a street vendor. "Isn't that Senator Hampton?"

Laurel's gaze followed her sister's finger. Sure enough, Eric Hampton stood on the stage, preparing to participate in the ceremony to crown the Cherry Blossom Queen. Seeing him brought a rush of memories, both sweet and bittersweet.

Eric was as handsome as ever, his strong jaw line and wide shoulders visible from a distance. He'd grown a beard since Laurel had seen him last. It was closely trimmed, a rich, chestnut brown color with a hint of red when the light hit it just right. He looked every bit the part of a respectable sena-tor. He had one of those trustworthy faces.

Della Brady, Laurel's friend and another Special Agent in Charge at the Bureau, arrived at that moment, her presence adding a layer of complexity to the situation. She greeted the group warmly, but Laurel could sense the underlying tension. Eric was someone they had both cared for deeply, and now his presence stirred emotions that neither of them had fully resolved. It was a strange merging of people and place.

"That's him," Laurel confirmed, after giving Della a quick hug. "He still looks good. The stress of being a U.S. Senator hasn't aged him too much."

Della raised her brow. "I'm not sure I agree. I had him first, and he's got more mileage on him as compared to those days. *Our* days."

It was a tricky subject between the friends. Della had dated Eric first. Laurel had dated him months later, although they'd never pieced that fact together until one day when Laurel and Eric had run into Della at a cafe in Georgetown. Both relationships had been serious. Della had spent the better part of two years with the now-senator. Laurel had spent one.

"Easy girls," Brad said with a smile.

Brad knew the story. He wasn't the jealous type, and he was easy going about Laurel's former relationships. That didn't mean he didn't care, though. He intended to be sure his fiancé remembered whom she was going home to at night.

"Why do I feel like there's a story here? Are we missing something?" Maggie asked, tossing her long, red hair over one shoulder. The humidity was making it curl more than usual.

"I'll fill you in later," Mikey said.

As the second oldest and the closest in age to Laurel, Mikey was often privy to more information about his big sister's life than the younger siblings were.

Maggie nodded, happy enough with her brother's response. "Thanks."

As the ceremony began, the crowd's attention shifted to the stage. Eric was in his element, charming and poised, as he spoke to the audience. Laurel couldn't help but feel a pang of admiration for him, mixed with the inevitable what-ifs.

Suddenly, though, the atmosphere changed.

Della's phone rang, and she answered it with a furrowed brow. Jimmy's phone rang, too, which set off alarm bells for Laurel. If both Special Agents in Charge were being called at the same time, something serious must be happening. Della's expression shifted from confusion to shock, and then to panic.

"What's going on?" Brad asked, concern evident in his voice.

Laurel shook her head, her own worry mounting. "I don't know, but it looks serious."

Answering their question, Jimmy covered the speaker on his phone with one hand long enough to whisper, "The senator's son has been kidnapped."

Two

DELLA ABSENTMINDEDLY TIGHTENED the band holding her long, brown hair in a ponytail. She listened carefully to the instructions coming from Headquarters, but she needed to do something with her hands.

"Why are there suddenly so many kidnappings?" she asked as she ended the call and returned her phone to her pants pocket.

"I don't know," Laurel said. "Where was the child taken from?"

"Where do you think?"

Laurel's eyes grew wide as the realization set in. "Do you mean ... Eric's son?"

Della nodded. "Unfortunately, yes. Billy Hampton. The boy is only four. He was taken from the yard of the family's home in Appleman's Gap, Tennessee while his mom, Sylvia, washed dishes inside. She claims she only looked away for a minute."

Saying it out loud made Della feel physically ill.

When you date someone for two whole years, you come

to care about them deeply. Even though she and Eric had broken up and he'd gone on to meet and marry Sylvia, she wished nothing but the best for him. She certainly didn't want to see him go through the anguish and terror that he'd now face. Her heart broke for her old flame.

Laurel felt much the same way.

"Oh, my God," Laurel said. "The Cradler. It has to be. But why Eric?"

Brad was nearby, listening closely. As Chief of Police in Appleman's Gap, it was his job to keep tabs on such matters. He hadn't heard from any of his officers yet. Perhaps they'd all grown so accustomed to the recent kidnappings in the area that they'd immediately turned things over to the F.B.I. Given the likelihood that The Cradler's syndicate was behind this abduction, they would have been right to do so. The Bureau would be lead, anyway.

Della shrugged. "Maybe there's a political motivation. Or maybe they just wanted a target in the public eye. This ceremony is being broadcast live, all over the country. Probably all over the world, in some form or another."

"Does he know?" Laurel asked as she eyed Eric from a distance. Instinctively, she put a hand over her pregnant belly.

"Doesn't seem like it," Brad replied.

"Doesn't seem like it to me, either," Della said. "The poor guy."

Just then, Jimmy finished his call and hung up the phone. He motioned to Della. "We've got to go," he said. "We've been told to accompany the Senator. He has to be questioned."

Della nodded, then moved to join Jimmy.

"What do I do?" Laurel asked.

Jimmy didn't hesitate. "Stay with your family and get your things moved home. We have this covered for now. We'll be in touch."

Laurel had arranged to continue working for the F.B.I., but from her hometown. No one was sure if that arrangement would be permanent, but for now, there was plenty to do in Middle Tennessee as law enforcement worked to bring The Cradler and his syndicate to justice.

Della looked at her friend, feeling helpless. The decision to involve Laurel in the investigation was beyond Della's pay grade. At least, it was until she learned more about the kidnapping and who the Bureau was assigning to investigate. Even then, Jimmy was the senior agent.

"Go," Della said, giving Laurel a quick hug. "We'll catch up soon. It was good to see you. Good to see you all."

Laurel squeezed her friend tightly, then whispered in her ear. "Tell him I'm sorry, okay? When you see him."

Della pulled back, a look of confusion on her face. "Sorry for what?"

"Just tell Eric. He'll understand."

They parted, then Della and Jimmy rushed toward the stage, hands on their service weapons. As they moved, some people in the crowd noticed the urgency. Della and Jimmy picked up their pace as they neared the Senator. Not only did they want to question him as soon as possible, but they wanted to be sure he was protected, in case he was a target, too. There were still too many unknowns to take chances.

Laurel and her family watched from a distance as the scene unfolded into chaos.

"So much for a relaxing evening at the Cherry Blossom Festival," Hazel said, shooting Laurel a dirty look.

"Yeah, let's hit the Metrorail before it gets mobbed," Mikey said. "I'd like to get back to our hotel in one piece. Who knows what kind of mass hysteria will take hold around here?"

Everyone agreed except Maggie, who seemed interested in staying to watch the drama unfold.

"Do we have to go?" she asked. "This is already more interesting than anything I've seen back home in Appleman's Gap. Like, ever."

The fact that her sister was making light of the situation didn't sit well with Laurel, but she understood where Maggie was coming from. Their hometown was a sleepy place in the hills of Tennessee. Usually, nothing much happened there. The group insisted that it was time to go, though, and Maggie reluctantly followed along as they made their way to a nearby rail station. A crowd on edge could quickly spiral out of control, which was a fact that Laurel and Brad knew all too well. Their priority was getting the family out of there. Besides, the professionals on duty had it covered. Brad and the Danes exited the chaotic scene.

By the time Della climbed the steps to the stage, a security guard had Eric by the arm and was ushering him off in the other direction. Della's heart pounded as she climbed the steps to the stage. Seeing Eric in the midst of this crisis felt surreal, as if the past and present were colliding in a way she had never anticipated.

The security guard was leading Eric away, but he looked back, confused. Della and Jimmy reached him just as he was about to speak.

"Mr. Hampton, we need to get you to a secure location," Jimmy said firmly, his hand on Eric's shoulder. "Your son has been kidnapped."

Eric's face went pale. "Billy? Oh my God, no." He looked at Della, seeking answers and comfort.

There was a complicated history between Della and Eric, especially when it came to the topic of children. Ultimately, it had led to their breakup, and Della's feelings were still hurt. It had been the better part of four years since the former couple had seen each other. Even then, the last time was in passing when Eric had recently become a new dad.

"We're going to do everything we can to find him," Della assured her former love, her voice steady despite the turmoil inside. "But we need to move now. You might be in danger as well. We can't take anything for granted until we know more."

Eric nodded, and the pain in his eyes was hard to witness. It seemed as if this cut him to the very core. As if his worst fear was coming true.

"I'm so sorry," Della mouthed.

He nodded slightly, an almost imperceptible motion of the chin.

"Let's go," Jimmy urged.

They quickly led Eric through the crowd and to a nearby SUV, the senator moving in a daze. Della stayed close, her protective instincts in overdrive. She couldn't let anything happen to Eric. Not now. Not ever. She rode in the back next to him while Jimmy drove. She wasn't about to leave him alone right now.

The ride to F.B.I. headquarters was tense. Eric hunched over the center console, his hands trembling. Della watched him, her heart aching for the man she had once loved deeply. If she was being completely honest with herself, she still did.

"Sylvia?" Eric asked, his expression pleading. His voice broke at the end of his wife's name.

"She's okay," Della replied, smiling with closed lips.

As Della thought about the woman who had become Mrs. Hampton, memories of the time she'd spent with Eric flooded her mind. They had been so good together. Their shared laughter, late-night conversations, and the painful day he'd ended things between them felt so fresh, they might as well have happened yesterday.

The passing years had done little to soothe Della's pain.

Eric had wanted children, and Della couldn't give him that. The breakup had left a scar on her heart that had never fully healed. But now wasn't the time to dwell on the past. She had to stay focused, to be the agent he needed her to be. The agent that young Billy Hampton needed her to be. The boy was innocent in all of this.

Della leaned closer, placing a reassuring hand on Eric's forearm. "Listen, the Bureau is good at this. You're in capable hands, okay? I want you to focus on a positive outcome. Don't let the what-ifs drag you down. Can you do that ... for me?"

Jimmy eyed his colleague through the rearview mirror. Her approach was too personal. He didn't know the history between Della and the Senator, but he was getting the idea that there was one.

"For you ... I guess," Eric replied reluctantly.

Della patted his arm, then traced a line up to his elbow with one finger.

"Everything okay back there, Agent Brady?" Jimmy asked. His tone was a warning.

Della pulled her hand back, then sat up straighter and smoothed the hem of her black pants. She shot Eric a look that let him know she'd be there for him, but that they'd need to play by the rules when other people were watching.

"Fine," Della replied. "I'm briefing the Senator on what to expect."

Jimmy looked skeptical. "We'll do that at Headquarters," he said tersely.

Della nodded her understanding. *Message received.* Still, she intended to handle this case the way she saw fit. It was too important to do otherwise.

Three

LAUREL and her family sat together on the Metrorail, the rhythmic clacking of the train providing a soothing backdrop. The cityscape of Washington, D.C., blurred past the windows. The city that had been Laurel's home for so many years now felt both familiar and distant.

Brad sat next to her, his arm wrapped protectively around her shoulders. Across from them, Mikey, Maggie, Hazel, and Ryan chatted animatedly, their voices a comforting hum. It was a rare occasion to have them all together, and despite the day's chaos and the unsettling news about Eric's son, Laurel cherished these moments.

Her thoughts drifted to the many memories she had made in D.C. She had arrived as a young woman with big dreams, and now she was leaving as a seasoned F.B.I. agent, soon-to-be wife, and soon-to-be mother. The city had witnessed her highest highs and lowest lows. She had met Brad here, fallen in love with him, and built a life she was proud of. Yet, the pull of Appleman's Gap, with its rolling hills and close-knit community, had always been there, tugging at her heart-strings.

Laurel thought about Eric, his wife, and their young son, Billy, who had been snatched by nefarious hands just hours before. Things could have been so different, had she and Eric stayed together. They'd both wanted families, and here they were, each moving forward in that direction. Only Eric's family had been ripped apart by a madman. Laurel's heart hurt for him. It could have been her who'd mothered Eric's child. Her son, taken. The realization made her shudder.

"Laurel, you okay?" Maggie's voice broke through. "Are you sad that the festival got interrupted? I know you were looking forward to showing us everything. The blossoms really are beautiful."

Laurel smiled, nodding. "It is a bummer that the festivities had to end early. And of course, I'm worried sick for Eric and his family. They must be terrified right now. Especially young Billy. I can't imagine what he's going through. Mostly, though, I'm thinking about how much has changed."

Brad squeezed Laurel's shoulder, offering his support. No one said it out loud, but they all knew that Laurel had been about Billy's age when she'd been kidnapped as a child. The connections were twisted. Complicated.

"I get it," Mikey said softly.

Brad leaned over and kissed Laurel gently on the forehead. After the stress of the day, Laurel looked forward to climbing into bed at the hotel and sinking deeper into his arms. She needed to feel safe and loved. Brad's embrace always did the trick, but it was best in private, away from the watchful eyes of others.

Hazel leaned forward, a mischievous glint in her eye. "So,

have you two set a date for the wedding yet? I know you're both itching to tie the knot before the baby arrives."

Brad squeezed Laurel again. "We've talked about it. It's just a matter of finding the right time. Things have been ... hectic, to say the least."

"That's an understatement," Mikey mused.

Laurel nodded. "Yeah, with everything going on with The Cradler and all. I want to focus on bringing him down. But I also don't want to wait too long. I want to marry you, Brad, more than anything."

Now that she knew Jamie Beck wasn't a threat, Laurel was truly ready to take the next step with her longtime love. There was nothing standing in their way, other than professional obligations. Those could be managed. Couldn't they?

Brad chuckled. "Are you saying you want me to make an honest woman out of you before the baby gets here?"

Laurel swatted at him playfully. "I'm not sure I think about it in those terms, exactly, but yes, Brad Tate. Make an honest woman out of me."

"Yeah?" Brad asked jovially. "We could find a minister right now. I'm sure there's one around here somewhere. Don't tempt me with a good time."

"No, silly," Laurel said. "Not without my parents."

Brad nodded, then kissed his fiancé again, on the lips this time. "I know," he said. "They'll be there. When it's time."

Ryan grinned. "We could always throw together a quick wedding in Appleman's Gap. The whole town would show up. You know how they love an excuse to celebrate."

Laurel chuckled. "True. But I want it to be special, not just a rushed affair."

Mikey chimed in. "Special doesn't have to mean elaborate.

We could do something beautiful and intimate, just close family and friends. And then, once the baby is here and things settle down, you could have a bigger celebration."

Brad looked thoughtful. "That could work. What do you think, Laurel?"

Laurel smiled, her heart swelling with love for the man beside her. "I think it sounds perfect. Tell me more."

As they discussed potential dates and venues, the conversation naturally shifted to Cornelius. Laurel's father had been a central figure in her life, and his recent reappearance had brought a mix of emotions.

"I mean, if having our dad return from the dead isn't special, I don't know what is," Ryan added. "He ought to be well enough now to walk you down the aisle, Sis. I can just see you, all dressed in white, on Dad's arm. It's a beautiful vision."

"You're wearing white?" Brad asked playfully.

"Why wouldn't I?" Laurel replied.

"Just asking. Because ... you know," Brad said, gesturing to Laurel's big belly. It had grown far too large to be called a baby bump.

"Stop it," Laurel said. "That's old fashioned, Brad. We're not like that."

Brad nodded. "I know. Just teasing you, babe." He kissed her again, lingering this time.

Maggie sighed, debating whether to tell her sister and soon-to-be brother-in-law to get a room. "How's Dad doing? I know he's staying in the pool house, but it must be weird with Mack still living in the main house with Mom. I've been so busy lately that I haven't been over to check on them."

Laurel nodded, returning her focus to her siblings. "It is

weird. Dad's recovering, thanks in large part to Alejandro, his physical therapist. That man's a miracle worker. But it's slow. Mom is keeping a close eye on him. She's always been good at that, taking care of everyone. It's just ... different now."

Ryan frowned. "Do you think it's awkward for him? Being so close but not really ... there? It's clear that he still loves Mom and wants them to get back together."

Ryan was on spring break from school at Middle Tennessee State University, but he'd be returning to Murfreesboro as soon as they all got back. He had missed out on a lot of the day-to-day happenings in Appleman's Gap over the past few years. He'd soon begin his career as a professional pilot after graduation, so it was unlikely that he'd settle in their hometown. Settling near a major airport like BNA in Nashville made good sense. At least, if he chose Nashville, he wouldn't be too far from the rest of the family.

Laurel shrugged. "It probably is awkward. But I think Dad understands that it's complicated. Mom and Mack have their own thing going on, and he doesn't want to disrupt that. At the same time, he needs to be near us, especially after everything that's happened. And it is still his home, technically."

Hazel sighed. "The whole town knows he's back. It was on national news. But people are keeping their distance, out of respect or maybe uncertainty. It's like they don't know how to approach him after thinking he was dead for so long."

Brad nodded. "It'll take time. People need to adjust. But the important thing is, he's back, and he's recovering. We just need to give him the space and support he needs. From what I can tell, his puppy is helping, too. Cornelius loves that Sully dog something fierce. I'm glad they have each other."

Laurel leaned her head against Brad's shoulder, feeling a wave of gratitude for her family and the love they shared. "Me, too. Look, we'll get through this. All of it. I don't know about you, but I'm counting my blessings right now that we aren't in Eric Hampton's position. I feel so badly for him. We need to find Billy and bring him home safely, like we did Jasper and Alexia."

"I agree, one hundred percent," Brad said.

"I second that," Mikey said.

"Same," the others said, practically in unison.

As the train continued its journey, Laurel allowed herself to relax. There wasn't anything she could do for Billy tonight, anyway. Della and Jimmy were on the case, and they were more than capable of covering the bases.

The conversation shifted to lighter topics, with Hazel teasing Ryan about his latest crush and Maggie sharing funny anecdotes from her business. She always met the strangest people in her work rehabbing and repurposing furniture. The atmosphere was warm and filled with laughter, a perfect contrast to the day's earlier tension.

When the train stopped at their station and they stepped off, the hotel coming into view, Laurel took a deep breath and savored the crisp evening air. Tomorrow, they would begin their journey back to Appleman's Gap, to a new chapter filled with hope and possibility.

Brad leaned over and whispered in Laurel's ear. "I have a surprise for you. It's in our room. I think you're going to love it."

Her cheeks pinked and a warmth moved through her as she considered the possibilities.

Four

WHEN DELLA, Eric, and Jimmy arrived at Headquarters, the sun had set and there was a chill in the air. Cool wind rustled through the American flags affixed to the front of the iconic J. Edgar Hoover F.B.I. Building. It was a reminder that it could still get quite cold this time of year.

Hopefully, it was warmer in Tennessee, where Billy was. Della was no expert on kids, but she knew enough to wish that the boy did not get too cold. From what she understood, kids couldn't tolerate those discomforts as easily as adults. Her experience with nieces and nephews had proven that to be true. She hoped Billy wasn't hungry, either.

Della opened her mouth to ask Jimmy if The Cradler was known for providing basic comforts for the kids he'd taken in the past, but she stopped herself. Eric was listening, and she didn't want to cause him any more distress. Besides, she already knew the answer to that question. Unfortunately, The Cradler and his goons didn't seem to care about comforts, as long as the kids were kept alive long enough to be of use. When the team that raided Ruth Patterson's place had found

Baby Alexia, the infant had been malnourished and suffering from hypothermia.

The thought made Della cringe. She had to look away to hide her reaction. *Poor Billy*, she thought. No child deserved this fate. Even if he was rescued soon, he'd be forever changed.

Once inside the dimly lit halls, Della and Jimmy quickly moved Eric to a secure room.

"This place looks just like it did on *The X-Files*," Eric said as they walked the halls. "Here I thought that was all fake. Makes me wonder what else was real."

The reference caused Della to blush. When she and Eric had been a couple, *The X-Files* had been one of their favorite guilty pleasures. They'd watched all nine original seasons, plus the two feature films and the more recent tenth and eleventh seasons. Suffice to say, they had been big fans. Mention of their pastime took Della right back. She could practically hear the familiar theme song and smell the microwave popcorn Eric had always popped for the occasion.

Della didn't respond, other than to smile.

Once Eric was situated, the agents joined a team already assembled, the urgency of the situation palpable.

"Let's go over what we know," Jimmy said, addressing the group. "Billy Hampton, four years old, was taken from his family's yard in Appleman's Gap, Tennessee. His mother was inside the house at the time, watching him through a window. She claims she only stepped away briefly. We believe The Cradler's syndicate is behind this."

"How could it not be?" Della asked. "This has The Cradler written all over it. We already know he operates in

Middle Tennessee, and he seems to have a particular fondness for Appleman's Gap."

Jimmy nodded. "He certainly does. At this point, it feels like he's taunting us."

Della's phone buzzed with new information, and she glanced at the screen. "We have a preliminary description of the suspect," she said. "A man in his mid-thirties, seen near the Hampton residence shortly before the abduction. We need to get this out to all local and national law enforcement agencies immediately. Has an Amber Alert been issued?"

"On it," an agent called from the back of the room.

The team sprang into action, disseminating the information and coordinating efforts. Della watched them, a mix of pride and determination filling her. They were a well-oiled machine, and she was confident they would find Billy ... eventually. Who knew how long it would take, though?

As they worked, Eric was prepped for questioning. Even though no one thought he was involved in his son's disappearance, he'd need to be cleared.

When Della rejoined him in the interrogation room, his face was drawn, eyes hollow with worry. She sat beside him, offering a reassuring presence. They waited together as Jimmy finished a phone call.

"Hami, we'll need to know everything," she said gently. "Anything you can think of that might help us find Billy. Even if it seems irrelevant, it could help."

He nodded, his voice shaky. He didn't seem to register that Della had just used a pet name. She had called him Hami when they were lovers.

"I don't know. I haven't talked to Sylvia. I don't understand how this happened," he said.

"We'll figure it out," Della said. "We have the best people on this. You have to trust me."

Eric looked at her, searching for comfort. He moved to reach for her, then stopped short. He raised a hand to cover his mouth instead. "I'm sorry for being such a mess," he said. "I'm in shock."

Eric's apology hung in the air, a stark reminder of the vulnerability that even a seasoned politician could feel in the face of personal tragedy. Della thought again how the stress seemed to have aged him. She placed a hand on his arm, her touch gentle but grounding. "You don't need to apologize. Anyone would be in shock after what you've been through."

That reminded Della. Laurel had asked her to give Eric a message. Now seemed as good a time as any. She leaned close and spoke softly.

"Laurel asked me to tell you that she's sorry."

He recoiled, surprised. "She's sorry? For what?"

Then it dawned on him, and his face fell. "Oh," he said simply.

Della began to ask questions, but Eric shook his head. Respecting his wishes, she moved on.

"Okay, then," she said. "I'll let what's between you and Laurel stay there. That love triangle is one that doesn't need to be revisited."

He nodded, his eyes filled with unshed tears. "I just ... I can't believe this is happening to Billy. He's so young."

Della's heart ached for him. She wanted to say more, to offer him some kind of solace, but words felt inadequate. Instead, she focused on the task at hand. "We're going to find him. We will."

They sat in silence for a moment. It was as if the years had melted away, and they were back to the days when they had leaned on each other for support, dreams of a future together still fresh and untainted by the reality of their divergent paths.

"Do you think it's political?" Eric asked, breaking the silence. His voice was hoarse, each word laced with fear and suspicion. "I never would have gone into this line of work, if I'd known. No job is worth risking my son's safety."

Della hesitated. "It's possible. The timing and your visibility certainly make it seem like it could be. We're looking into every angle."

Eric's expression hardened. "You have to clear me as a suspect, don't you?"

Della looked away, the necessity of her duty clashing with her personal feelings. "Yes. It's protocol. We have to rule out every possibility."

Eric let out an exasperated laugh. "Of course. Just do what you need to do."

Della felt frustrated, both at the situation and at the distance that had grown between them. "It's not because we think you're guilty. It's because we need to be thorough. The faster we clear you, the faster we can focus on finding Billy."

He looked at her, his eyes softening. "I know, D. I know. It's just ... hard."

She nodded, understanding all too well the complexities of their past. When they had been together, the future had seemed so bright. They had talked about marriage, about having children, and about building a life together. But when Della discovered she couldn't have children, it had shattered those dreams. She had been willing to adopt, but Eric had wanted his own biological children. It was a divide they couldn't bridge.

Now, sitting beside him, the pain of that time came rushing back. She had wished so desperately to give him what he wanted. To be the person he needed. In the end, it hadn't been enough. And now, here they were, thrown back together by circumstances neither of them could control.

"Do you ever think about what might have been?" Eric asked softly, his voice barely above a whisper.

Della's heart twisted. "Sometimes," she admitted. "But we can't dwell on the past. We have to focus on the present."

Eric nodded, his eyes full of unspoken regrets. "You're right. I just wish things had been different."

Della squeezed his arm gently. "So do I."

Their eyes locked, and for a second, the years melted away. They were just two people, caught in a storm of emotions and memories, struggling to make sense of it all. Eric's hand found Della's, and he held on tightly, as if drawing strength from her presence.

Jimmy entered the room, breaking the moment. "We're ready to start," he said, glancing between them. "Senator Hampton, we need to ask you some questions to clear you as a suspect. It's standard procedure."

Eric nodded, letting go of Della's hand. "I understand. Let's get this over with."

The interrogation began, and Della took a step back, observing as Jimmy went through the necessary questions. She watched Eric closely, noting his reactions, his body language. He was cooperative, but the strain was evident.

As the questions continued, Della's mind wandered. She thought about her own life, about the paths she had taken and the dreams she had left behind. She had poured herself into her career, finding purpose and fulfillment in her work.

But there was always a part of her that longed for something more, something she had never been able to have.

She had never known her biological father, and the mystery of his identity had always been a shadow in her life. Her mother had been vague about him, and Della had never pressed too hard, not wanting to reopen old wounds. Now, with Eric's pain laid bare before her, she felt a renewed urgency to uncover her own past. She wanted to understand where she came from.

The desire for family ties and a sense of belonging was a deep ache within her. The fact that she couldn't have her own children had been a devastating blow, one that had ultimately pushed Eric away. The longing and the heartbreak they had felt during those years they were together had been too much for him to bear.

Della couldn't blame him for backing away.

When the interrogation was over, Eric looked exhausted. Jimmy left the room to process the information, leaving Della and Eric alone once more.

"Thank you for being here," Eric said quietly. "I don't know what I would do without you."

"You don't have to thank me, Hami. I'll always be here for you."

He reached out again, taking her hand in his. "I'm sorry for everything that happened between us. I wish ... I truly wish things could have been different."

Della squeezed his hand. "So do I. More than you know."

Eric nodded, his eyes searching hers. "I don't want to lose you again. Will you stick around?"

She felt a lump in her throat, emotions threatening to overwhelm her. "You won't lose me. I promise."

In that moment, the walls between them seemed to crumble.

Without thinking, Della leaned in, her lips brushing his cheek in a tender kiss. It was a kiss filled with years of unspoken words and unresolved feelings. A kiss that bridged the gap between their past and their present.

When she finally pulled away, they were both breathless. Eric rested his forehead against hers, his voice a whisper. "I love you, D."

Tears filled Della's eyes. "I love you too, Hami. Always have and always will."

Five

"KEEP YOUR EYES CLOSED," Brad insisted as he led Laurel out of the elevator and down the hall to their hotel room. "No peeking, Laurel Dane. I mean it."

"Is this really necessary?" she asked with a giggle. "If whatever you have for me is in our room, why do my eyes have to be closed now? Won't the door hide the surprise?"

"Because I can't be too careful with you, Miss F.B.I. agent-lady," he replied.

She shook her head, happy to go along with his game.

The rest of the Dane siblings had been assigned to rooms on the same floor, but they had mysteriously vanished downstairs in the lobby. Laurel assumed that Brad had instructed them to allow the couple some privacy. Or maybe they were in on whatever this was and they'd gone to their duty stations. The thought made Laurel even more curious to know what Brad had planned.

Finally, they reached the door. Brad carefully maneuvered Laurel inside, guiding her steps with gentle hands on her shoulders. "Okay, babe, you can open your eyes now," he said, excitement in his voice.

Laurel blinked her eyes open and gasped. There, laid out on the bed, was her French horn, polished to a gleam, and a long, elegant black dress. The sight took her breath away.

"What is this?" she asked, touching the dress' soft fabric. "Brad, what's going on? I could have sworn I put my horn on the moving truck. I made sure to put it in its hard case and place it in a secure location. Not to mention, it wasn't this shiny earlier."

He smiled, his eyes twinkling with delight. "I've got one last gig for you. I reached out to some of your old Air Force Band colleagues. They would love to play with you again. So … you're performing at a fancy retirement community on the water tonight. They've prepared a wonderful dinner, and the residents are all dressed up, excited to hear some great music. I thought it would be a special way to say goodbye to D.C."

Laurel felt tears prick her eyes. "Babe, you're sweet, but I haven't played in months. Since getting pregnant, actually. I don't know if my lip is in shape for this."

Brad wrapped his arms around her, pulling her close. "The quintet is playing from the classic *Canadian Brass Book of Favorite Quintets*. You know that music like the back of your hand. It'll be like riding a bike. You can absolutely do this. And the baby might love it, too."

She laughed through her tears. "You've thought of everything, haven't you?"

"I tried," he admitted, kissing her forehead. "You've given up so much for us, for the move, for the baby. I wanted to give you something special. Something that's just for you."

Laurel took a deep breath, feeling the weight of her

worries lift. "Okay," she said. "Like riding a bike, huh? Let's do it."

Brad pulled her close, kissing her deeply. "I'm so damn proud of you," he said when they came up for air. "How did I get so lucky?"

Laurel smiled, running a hand down the front of his body, letting her fingers trail lightly against the bulge below his belt. "I don't know, but I suspect you might get even luckier later tonight."

He grinned, kissing her again. "Promise?"

She nodded enthusiastically. "Oh, yes. You can count on it."

The hours that followed were a whirlwind of preparation. Laurel slipped into the black dress, feeling a sense of nostalgia wash over her as she picked up her French horn. Brad put on a suit and tie then helped her with her hair and makeup, and soon they were ready to go. They met the rest of the Dane siblings downstairs. They were all dressed to the nines.

"Look at you, Sis," Mikey said, wiping a tear from his eye. "You're a vision."

"Aww, thanks, Mikey," Laurel said as she hugged her brother's neck.

"Gorgeous," Maggie echoed.

"Our sister, the talented beauty," Ryan added.

"Beautiful," Hazel said.

They all smiled, happy for the chance to be a part of something special.

"I wish Mom and Dad could be here, too," Laurel said.

Brad smiled knowingly. "Already covered."

"Seriously?"

"Well," he said, "they won't actually be here in person,

but I promised to record video for them. They said to tell you they're with you in spirit. And they sent you this ..."

Brad pulled a small box out of his coat pocket and presented it to Laurel.

"What is this?" she asked.

"Open it and find out," Mikey urged.

Laurel lifted the top, and her eyes went wide. Inside was a beautiful cocktail ring with a square-cut blue topaz at the center. Tiny diamonds lined the gold band.

Brad continued to explain. "They said that when you look at this ring, they want you to remember that you have *two* parents who love you."

"Aww," Laurel cooed.

A few months prior, she'd thought her dad was dead. Finding out he was alive had been the shock of her life, but a good one, at that. She'd been angry at first, but she'd soon learned that he'd faked his death so that he could work undercover to bring The Cradler's kidnapping syndicate down. There was still much more work to do, but Cornelius had made significant progress in the investigation. At this point, Laurel felt nothing but love and appreciation for all her dad had done. Not to mention, she hoped that her Mom could someday forgive him and that they'd get back together.

This gift and the message to go with it meant the world. She placed it on the ring finger of her right hand. It was a perfect fit.

"Thank you," Laurel said to Brad, "for delivering this gift and its message."

"My pleasure," Brad replied with a smile. "But that isn't all."

He rifled around in his pocket and pulled out similar

small boxes for Mikey, Maggie, Hazel, and Ryan. As they opened them, happy expressions covered their faces. In the boxes were cocktail rings for Maggie and Hazel and diamond cufflinks for Mikey and Ryan.

"Same message for you four," Brad said. "Remember that you have *two* parents who love you."

"This is almost too much," Ryan said, tearing up.

"Thanks for being the messenger, Brad," Mikey said, giving his friend and soon-to-be brother-in-law a firm pat on the back.

"My absolute pleasure."

The group took an Uber to the retirement community, and the drive there was filled with laughter. When they arrived, the staff welcomed them warmly, escorting them to a beautifully decorated hall where the residents were already gathered. Lights from boats dotted the surface of the water in the distance. The air buzzed with excitement.

Laurel's former bandmates greeted her with hugs and smiles, their camaraderie rekindling instantly. It had been years since Laurel had left the Air Force Band to pursue a career with the Bureau, but that didn't matter. Friends who had played beautiful music together were friends for life. Besides, the kind of musical talent Laurel was blessed with didn't just go away. Even if her chops were out of shape, she'd make sure no one knew it.

The quintet warmed up, the familiar notes bringing back a flood of memories for Laurel.

Her horn felt so right in her hands. It was as if it was an extension of her body. Another appendage that she couldn't very well live without. Holding it felt like home. Hearing the rich, warm notes emanating from her bell was like coming home to a warm meal and a crackling fire on a cold day. It truly was a balm for anything that ailed her.

Laurel felt the baby kick in response to the music, a joyful reaction that made her smile. She hadn't expected the baby to have much of an opinion, but it made sense. Perhaps the little one would be a musician, too.

When she turned to reach for a tissue to wipe her leaky eyes, Brad was already there with a crisp white handkerchief in hand.

"I thought you might need this," he said sweetly.

"You're the best," she whispered, taking the cloth and dabbing gently.

They were happy tears.

Soon, the performance began, and as they played the first notes of "Trumpet Voluntary," Laurel felt the music flow through her, filling her with a sense of peace and fulfillment. The sensation was undescribable to someone who hadn't experienced it for themselves, but to his credit, Brad tried his best to understand. Laurel's contentment deepened as they proceeded to play "Toreador Song," "Trumpet Tune and Ayre," and "Farandole."

The residents listened cheerfully, their faces lighting up with recognition and joy. That was the good thing about senior citizens in a retirement home—they were enthusiastic listeners. Laurel had performed for their demographic before, and she'd always loved it every bit as much as they had seemed to.

Her fingers moved effortlessly over the keys, the muscle memory returning as if she'd never stopped playing. She glanced at Brad, who stood at the side, watching her with pride and love. Her family, too, beamed at her, their support palpable.

When they played Pachelbel's Canon, Laurel practically wept. It had always been one of her favorites, probably because it reminded her of the beauty and the cycle of life.

As the music pulsed rhythmically and she looked over at Brad, she knew it was the piece she wanted played at their wedding. In fact, she wanted it played as she walked down the aisle. And she wanted her friends from the brass quintet to be the ones playing. She hoped they'd be up for a trip to Tennessee. The entire future scene came into clear focus.

After the song finished, she mouthed to Brad, "Our wedding."

He looked confused at first, then he got it. With a big smile and a nod, he was on board. He gave her a dorky thumbs up, which made Laurel laugh with delight.

"Gracious," she mused, resting a hand on her pregnant belly.

For that moment, at least, everything was right in her world. She said a silent prayer to the powers that be, thanking them for the good things in her life.

During a break between pieces, the Dane siblings took to the floor, dancing together and inviting the residents to join them. Laughter filled the room as everyone celebrated the evening. The chef had prepared a sumptuous meal, and the aromas of roasted meats, fresh vegetables, and decadent desserts wafted through the air.

This was an evening to remember.

As they played the final piece, "Sakura & Kimgayo"—a nod to the Cherry Blossom Festival, Laurel felt a wave of emotions.

The music, the setting, and the love surrounding her was all overwhelming. She thought of all the music she'd played in D.C. —the concerts, the ceremonies, the sense of purpose and pride it had given her. And now, as she prepared to leave this chapter behind, she realized that music would always be a part of her, just as D.C. would always hold a special place in her heart.

No one could take either away.

Not now. Not ever.

When the last note faded, the room erupted in applause. Laurel stood with her fellow musicians, then took a bow, tears streaming down her face. She stepped off the stage and into Brad's arms, holding him tightly.

"Thank you," she whispered. "This was perfect."

Brad kissed her gently. "Anything for you, my love. Anything."

They spent the rest of the evening dancing, eating, and celebrating with the residents and each other. It was a night filled with love and music. A perfect farewell to a city that had given Laurel so much.

As they headed back to the hotel, the baby moved again. Laurel placed a hand on her belly, feeling the warmth of Brad's hand covering hers.

She'd been so preoccupied the past few months, torn between her commitment to the F.B.I. and the allure of starting her own private investigation firm. Not to mention, planning for the wedding and the baby, plus checking in on Cornelius' recovery and keeping an eye on her Mom and Mack. She still wasn't sure she trusted that man. It seemed like it had been a long time since she'd let go and lived completely in the moment, like she had tonight.

"We're going to be okay," she said softly, looking up at Brad.

He smiled, his eyes shining with love. "Yes, we sure are."

She leaned her head against his shoulder, letting the warmth of his embrace and the memories of the night fill her heart.

She hoped Billy Hampton was somewhere safe, and that he'd soon be returned to his parents' loving arms.

IT TOOK SEVERAL HOURS, but Della finally received word that Eric was being released. She sat alone at her desk, looking through the case file, when Jimmy arrived with the news.

"I trust you'll keep an eye on him tonight Agent Brady," Jimmy said, a look of resignation on his face. He seemed to know that was a bad idea, but they were all tired and he wanted to go home to his bed. He was getting too old to burn the midnight oil.

"I can do that," Della replied, dabbing gently at the bags under her eyes. She tried her best to keep her tone even.

The thought of spending more time with Eric suddenly made her want to freshen up. The change of clothes in her gym bag would have to do. Too bad the yoga pants and t-shirt she had packed weren't more flattering.

"One of our profilers needs to interview him tomorrow morning, before he flies home to Tennessee," Jimmy explained. "In the meantime, though, he can leave here and get some rest. Stay away from his place. It's still being searched. Keep a low profile, okay?"

Della nodded, her mind already racing.

"Jimmy?" she asked as he walked away.

They were friends. She knew she could be honest with him.

"Yeah?"

"The Senator and I ... we used to ... well, we were once a couple," she said.

Jimmy sighed as he turned and leaned against the glass partition that provided a view to the common area. "I got that idea. Will it be a problem?"

Della was surprised, although not much. Jimmy was a perceptive guy. Besides, she knew that the spark between her and Eric was still there, and it was probably easy to see.

"No," she said firmly. "I'm a professional. This is my career. I won't do anything to jeopardize that. Frankly, my career is all I have."

Jimmy believed her, so he said his goodbyes and left.

Della quickly changed in the restroom, doing her best to make the casual outfit presentable. When she returned, Eric was waiting in the lobby, his shoulders slumped with exhaustion. She felt the urge to reach out for him, but she held herself back.

"You ready to get out of here?" she asked softly.

Eric looked up, his eyes meeting hers with a mixture of relief and gratitude. "More than ready," he replied. He chuckled when he saw her outfit. "Are we going to the gym?"

Della laughed, too. "It was the only change of clothes I had. Don't make fun. I had planned to be home in my jammies by now."

He smiled, glancing at her toned backside. "I don't mind. You're showing off one of my favorite ... assets."

She blushed as they left the building together, the cool night air biting at their skin. The sweet scent of the cherry tree blooms mingled with the smell of the Potomac, giving the air a distinctive aroma. Della loved this time of year in our nation's capital. From what she remembered, Eric did, too.

Della led him to her car, and they drove in silence for a while, the city lights flashing by like a blur of memories.

"Where are we going?" Eric asked finally, breaking the silence.

"I figured you could use a hot meal and some sleep," Della said, glancing over at him. "I booked you a room at a nearby hotel. It's nothing fancy, but it's comfortable. Forensics is still working at your place."

Eric nodded, his gaze distant. "Thanks, D. I realize I sound like a broken record, but I don't know what I'd do without you right now."

"No trouble at all," she replied. "Even though you are keeping me from my favorite TV shows."

He turned to look at her, and she could feel his eyes traveling the length of her petite frame. It was remarkable how easy they were falling into old patterns. Almost like they'd never been apart. Like they were a good pair.

They arrived at the hotel, and Della checked Eric in. He waited in the car until she sent him a text, instructing him to enter through a service entrance in the back. Della knew he didn't want to be recognized, so she'd given him one of Jimmy's Baltimore Orioles ballcaps as an added bit of disguise. It worked. No one looked twice at the senator who was now in the midst of a personal nightmare. As Della knew all too well, that nightmare had the potential to quickly become a very public scandal, depending on how things played out in the days to come.

As they rode the elevator to his floor, Della found herself hyper-aware of Eric's presence. The familiar scent of his cologne stirred memories she had tried to bury.

When they reached his room, he turned to her, his eyes searching hers. "Will you stay for a while? I don't think I can be alone right now."

Della hesitated, knowing how dangerous this could be. The look in his eyes was too much to resist. She nodded slowly. "Of course. I'll stay. I'm famished. Want to order in?"

He nodded, gratefully. "We can watch your favorite TV shows together."

"Maybe."

They entered the room, and Della closed the door behind them. The space was warm and inviting, a stark contrast to the cold, sterile environment of the F.B.I. headquarters. Two plush sofas adorned with pastel pink pillows flanked the sitting area. The color scheme was a perfect match to the cherry blossoms decorating the city.

Eric sank onto the edge of a sofa, his shoulders slumping further.

"I feel like my whole world is falling apart," he admitted, his voice barely above a whisper. "I've worked so hard to hold it all together."

Della sat beside him, placing a comforting hand on his back. "You're not alone, Eric. We'll find Billy, and we'll bring him home."

"It's more than just that."

Della looked at him, puzzled, but she didn't ask questions. What more could he be referring to? She knew life as a senator was stressful. Was that all?

He turned to face her. "You've always been there for me, even when things got tough."

Della felt her heart ache at his words. She *had* always been there for him, sometimes at her own detriment. It had never been enough. A wiser woman would have cut ties sooner. For that matter, a wiser woman would have asked Jimmy to escort Eric to his hotel room.

"I'll always be here for you," she said softly. "I'm not going anywhere."

Eric reached out, his hand brushing against Della's cheek. The touch sent a shiver down her spine, and she felt her resolve weakening. "You don't know how much that means to me," he said, his voice thick with emotion.

Their faces were inches apart, the tension between them electric. Della knew she should pull away, that this was a line they shouldn't cross. Eric was a married man.

Before she could think, his lips were on hers, the kiss tender and desperate all at once. He tasted like his favorite soda, root beer. It was a sensory detail she had forgotten but that now came rushing back. Della's heart pounded in her chest as she returned the kiss, her hands tangling in his hair.

It felt like coming home, like finding a piece of herself she had lost long ago.

But as the kiss deepened, reality crashed back in. Della pulled away, breathless and conflicted. "Hami, we can't ..."

He looked at her, his eyes filled with regret. "I know. I'm sorry. It's just ... everything is so messed up right now."

Della nodded, struggling to regain her composure. "I get it. I do. But this isn't the answer."

Eric sighed, running a hand through his hair. Della had always loved his hair. He kept it neat, but at five or six inches long, it was more unruly than the clean-cut men she typically dated. Something about it was almost wild.

"You're right," he said. "I just don't know what to do with myself."

Della reached out, squeezing his hand. "Have you called Sylvia?"

He looked at her. "No. I'm almost afraid to."

"Well, then, that's step number one. She must be worried sick. She'll want to hear from you."

Eric seemed reluctant, but he nodded. "I guess you're right."

He stood, lifting his phone and pushing a few buttons to dial Sylvia's number. Della stood, too, then ushered Eric into the adjoining bedroom to give him some privacy. When she heard ringing on the other end of the line, she closed the door gently, leaving him alone inside.

Feeling guilty, Della decided to reach out to Laurel. Perhaps her friend would have some sage advice, especially since she'd dated Eric, too. She probably understood how alluring that man could be. Della found Laurel's number and dialed, but it went right to voicemail.

"Of course," Della said to herself.

Laurel was with Brad and her siblings, spending her last night in D.C. She probably had her phone off. But Della wanted to talk to someone. Someone who understood what she'd been through. Quickly, she pressed a few buttons and Paloma Lopez was on the line.

"Mija? What's wrong?" the old woman asked as she answered.

"Mom, nothing's wrong," Della replied. She kept her voice low so as not to be overheard. "What makes you automatically assume something is wrong?"

"Call it a mother's intuition," Paloma said.

Della smiled. Her mom was right about that much. The woman had intuition, and it was honed when it came to her only daughter.

"How warm is it in San Antonio today? Is it still daylight there?" Della asked.

"It's dark, Mija. Now I know for sure something is wrong. You've lost track of time. Tell me."

Della exhaled heavily, then plopped down on a sofa. "Okay, you got me. I'm calling for some motherly advice."

"Go on."

"You remember Eric Hampton, right?"

Paloma shrieked on the other end of the line. "The weasel who broke your heart because you couldn't give him biological children? I remember too well. I'd like to give him a kick where the sun doesn't shine."

Paloma might not be sugar coating it, but she wasn't wrong.

"He just kissed me."

Seven

SOFT LIGHT SHONE from Laurel's laptop screen as she sat perched on a barstool in her hotel suite. She'd made passionate love to Brad to cap a truly memorable evening, but she'd found herself wide awake after he'd drifted off to sleep.

Call it an inability to separate work and personal life, but she wanted desperately to do something to help find Billy Hampton.

"That poor boy," she mused as she rubbed her pregnant belly.

She was still toying with the idea of opening a detective agency with her dad and Mikey, but for now, she was an F.B.I. agent with a duty to uphold. She intended to give it her all. Not to mention, she was protective of her hometown and didn't like seeing it on national news. The rash of kidnappings was giving the town a bad rep.

Laurel's fingers hovered over the keyboard as she contemplated logging into the F.B.I.'s secure server. She knew the protocols well. Years of training and experience had drilled them into her. Being in a hotel meant she had to be extra cautious, even with the high level of security the F.B.I.'s system already employed.

First, she plugged in the portable USB security key, a small device that acted as a second factor of authentication, ensuring that no one could access the system without it. Then, she activated the virtual private network (VPN), which encrypted her internet connection, shielding her activity from potential prying eyes. Finally, she used her fingerprint to unlock the secure application that would allow her access to the F.B.I. database. The system whirred to life, presenting her with a digital portal into the Bureau's extensive resources.

The screen displayed a list of ongoing cases, and Laurel quickly navigated to the one involving Billy Hampton. The case file opened before her, a mix of reports, suspect lists, and leads gathered from various sources. She felt a pang of sorrow as she saw the boy's innocent face in the attached photo. It reminded her of how vulnerable children could be and how easily they could be taken and used as pawns in someone else's game.

Laurel scanned the updates from earlier that day, her eyes narrowing as she read through the preliminary findings. Something caught her attention—a notation from one of the agents about Eric Hampton's recent financial activities. It seemed out of place, and her instinct told her to dig deeper.

Her fingers danced across the keyboard as she pulled up Eric's financial records. The FBI had already obtained a warrant to monitor his accounts, a necessary step to rule him out as a suspect. Laurel's heart sank as she noticed several large transfers of money, all made within the past few weeks. They were directed to offshore accounts, which immediately raised red flags. The amounts weren't typical of someone simply managing their finances. They were significant enough to suggest something more sinister.

Could Eric be involved?

The thought sent a chill down her spine. She'd known him as a man of integrity, someone who had always seemed to put his family and country first. But the evidence was unsettling. What would prompt a father, a U.S. Senator no less, to move such large sums of money in secret?

Laurel leaned back in her chair, her mind racing. She tried to imagine the circumstances that would lead Eric to be involved in something as heinous as the kidnapping of his own son. Was it political? Was he being blackmailed? Or was there something darker at play that she hadn't yet uncovered?

Her gaze drifted toward Brad, who was still sound asleep in the bed. The rhythmic rise and fall of his chest was comforting, but it didn't ease the turmoil inside her.

Should she tell Della? Could she really believe that Eric might be capable of something so monstrous?

Laurel knew that the Bureau's job was to follow the evidence wherever it led, no matter how uncomfortable it might be. But this was personal. She had once cared for Eric, and her dear friend, Della, had too. The thought of shattering the trust, of possibly betraying friends, made her hesitate. The feelings were complicated.

She glanced back at the screen, the damning evidence staring her in the face. This wasn't just a suspicion. It was something she had to act on. But how? What would she say? How could she break this to Della without causing her more pain?

Laurel closed her eyes, taking a deep breath to steady herself. She had to tread carefully, but she also had to do her duty. The conflict gnawed at her. The lines between right and wrong seemed blurred.

She picked up her phone, noticing it was still powered off from the quintet performance earlier in the evening. She turned it on, the screen slowly coming to life.

"That's weird," she said, seeing the missed call from Della. "She doesn't usually call this late."

Brad stirred, and Laurel knew she needed to get out of the room for a while so she didn't wake him up. Making a quick decision, she texted Mikey.

You awake?

His reply was instantaneous.

Yep. Can't sleep. What's up?

Meet me in the lobby in five.

Tiptoeing around the suite, she threw on sweatpants and a hoodie, then slid into her shoes and grabbed her handbag. She logged off the computer and put it away in her bag, then scribbled a note for Brad and tucked it under his phone on the nightstand.

Her brother was already seated in the hotel lounge near the bar when she arrived.

"Taking a pregnant lady to a bar now, are you?" she asked as she sat down.

"I'm doing no such thing," he said with a laugh. "You're the one who invited me."

"I didn't tell you to sit at the bar," Laurel said.

He leaned back and smiled as a server brought them two glasses of water.

"See?" Mikey asked. "Water."

"Okay, okay."

He took a big sip, then set the glass down with a clank. "What are we doing here, Sis? I thought you and Brad would be ... busy."

"Oh, we were busy all right," she said. "But then Brad conked out and I couldn't sleep."

"Let me guess. So you got to work on Billy Hampton's case?"

She nodded. "Something like that. You know me too well."

"I must admit, I was thinking it over, too," he replied. Mikey leaned in closer, his expression serious. "What did you find out?"

Laurel hesitated, her fingers tracing the rim of her water glass. "It's not good, Mikey. I dug into Eric's financials. There have been some significant transfers to offshore accounts, and they're recent. Within the last few weeks."

Mikey's brow furrowed. "Offshore accounts? That doesn't sound like something a U.S. Senator would need unless ..." He trailed off, not wanting to voice the implications.

Laurel nodded, finishing his thought. "Unless he's involved in something shady. It could be nothing. But it's enough to make me wonder if he had anything to do with Billy's kidnapping."

Mikey leaned back in his chair, absorbing the information. "Do you really think Eric could be capable of something like that? I mean, you knew him. Della did, too."

"That's what's so upsetting," Laurel admitted, her voice tinged with frustration. "The Eric I knew wouldn't do this. No way. But people change, and money—especially large sums—can make people do desperate things. I don't want to believe it, but I also can't ignore the evidence."

Mikey sighed, running a hand through his blonde hair. "This is a tough one, Sis. You've got to be careful. If you tell Della and it turns out to be nothing, it could destroy your friendship. She's obviously got a soft spot for the guy. I'm not sure she'll listen to reason. But if you don't tell her, and Eric is involved in something bad, you're letting a criminal walk free."

Laurel nodded. "I know. I keep going back and forth in my mind. Della called me earlier tonight, before I got to the case files. She never calls this late unless it's important. What if she found something, too? What if she's already onto Eric?"

Mikey looked thoughtful, his eyes narrowing. "It's possible. She's a sharp agent, just like you. But if she suspects something and hasn't told you, it could mean she's trying to protect you. Or maybe even protect Eric."

Laurel's stomach churned at the thought. "I don't know if I can sit on this information. I also don't want to jump to conclusions. I need to be sure before I say anything."

Mikey reached across the table, placing his hand on hers. "You don't have to decide right now. Let's take a step back and think it through."

Knowing she had Mikey's support was a relief to Laurel. He'd offered his hacking help on multiple occasions, but she hadn't taken him up on it. Perhaps it was time. If they were going to work together in an agency at some point, they might as well get started collaborating.

Just as she began to relax, Laurel's phone buzzed on the table, startling them both. She picked it up, her heart skipping a beat when she saw it was Della calling again.

"So much for ordering food," Mikey mused.

Laurel hesitated for a moment, exchanging a look with Mikey before answering. "Della? What's going on?"

There was no answer. The line went dead.

Laurel hung up, her pulse quickening as she turned to Mikey. "Something's wrong. I can feel it. We need to go."

Mikey didn't waste a second, grabbing his jacket and following Laurel out of the lounge.

BY THE TIME Paloma got tired of the conversation with her daughter and made an excuse to get off the phone, Eric had finished the call with his wife. He returned to the sitting area of the suite. Della turned her attention to him, happy to see that he appeared relieved. He had changed into sweats and a Pink Floyd t-shirt that Jimmy had given him to wear. The clothes were a size too small, but they did a nice job highlighting Eric's muscular physique.

"How did it go?" Della asked.

She was seated on a sofa, her legs curled lazily underneath her and a pink pillow on her lap. Talking to her mom had helped. Even though Paloma wasn't a fan of Eric Hampton's, she had encouraged her daughter to trust her gut and put herself first. It was good advice.

Eric sat down across from Della and exhaled a deep breath. He looked exhausted, the day's events clearly taking a toll on him.

Della appreciated that he was sitting on a different piece of furniture. She wasn't sure how well she could resist his charms, if he sat any closer. He was a handsome man, and the two of them were still very attracted to each other.

"It went as well as could be expected, I suppose," Eric said, rubbing a hand over his bearded face. The mature, bearded look suited him. "Sylvia is worried, of course, but she's holding herself together. She's always been good at that—putting on a brave face, especially when the cameras are rolling."

Della nodded, sensing there was more he wasn't saying. She'd known Eric long enough to recognize when something was bothering him, even if he was trying to hide it.

"You know you can talk to me," she said. "If there's something else going on, something you want to get off your chest …"

He hesitated, his eyes flickering with uncertainty before meeting hers. "It's complicated. Things between Sylvia and me haven't been right for a long time."

Della stiffened. "What do you mean? Is there trouble in your marriage?"

She almost felt bad to ask, but she honestly wanted to know. Perhaps a small part of her wished for her old flame to be available again. She wasn't seeing anyone. In fact, she hadn't been involved in a serious relationship since the two of them had broken up.

Eric sighed, leaning back on the cushion and staring at the ceiling as if searching for the right words. "We haven't had a real marriage in years. It's all for appearances. For the sake of the public. Sylvia and I, we're more like business partners at this point. We stay together because it's what's expected of us. A divorce would be political suicide, and she knows that just as well as I do. She enjoys a certain lifestyle and status. She needs me for that."

Della's brow furrowed in concern. "You're saying you're staying together just to keep up the facade? That sounds unbearable."

He looked back at her, his expression one of resignation. "It really is, but I made my bed, didn't I? I chose this life. The career. The public scrutiny. I have to live with the consequences."

Della felt a pang of sympathy for him. Eric had always been ambitious, driven by a desire to make a difference. But she had never imagined the personal sacrifices he had made to maintain his position. The thought of him being trapped in a loveless marriage, all for the sake of appearances, hurt her heart.

It shouldn't have to be this way. How had things gone so wrong?

"I'm sorry, Hami," she said softly. "I can't imagine how difficult that must be for you. Sometimes, I feel sorry for myself because I'm lonely, but I guess I'd rather be lonely than in a situation like yours."

He gave a half-hearted smile, one that didn't quite reach his eyes. "It is what it is, I suppose. But there are times when I wonder what might have been if I had chosen differently."

Della's breath caught in her throat at his words. "I've wondered the same thing," she admitted, her voice barely above a whisper. "Did we give up on each other too quickly?"

Eric's gaze softened as he looked at her. "Maybe? I don't know. I've missed you, D. More than I can say."

She leaned forward. "I've missed you, too," she said.

It occurred to Della that this was how it happened. This was how people had affairs. It wasn't that they were bad people. They were lonely people, looking to fill the hole of whatever was missing in their lives. The urge to act on the impulse was almost too much to resist, especially in a situation like this where there was a complicated history. Everything else seemed to fade away. All of their obligations and responsibilities seemed irrelevant in this moment. After all, they were alone in this hotel room. No one would see or know what happened behind the closed door.

Eric leaned closer, his eyes locked on hers. Della's breath hitched as she felt him move toward her, the space between them shrinking until she could feel the warmth of his breath on her skin.

Just as their lips were about to meet, the sound of a knock on the door jolted them both back to reality. Della pulled away, her heart pounding in her chest as the moment was shattered.

Eric cleared his throat, standing up quickly and moving toward the door. Della straightened herself, trying to regain her composure.

"I'll get it," Eric said. "Probably the food we ordered."

"Did you put an order in?" Della asked. She didn't realize he'd done so.

"Yeah, while I was in the other room. I got us Capital Tacos, your old favorite. You still like them, right?"

She nodded. "Yeah, that will hit the spot."

When Eric opened the door, though, there was no one there. Just an empty hallway and the soft echo of footsteps retreating down the corridor. He frowned, looking back at Della with confusion.

"Must have been a false alarm," he said. "I'll double check delivery time on the app."

Della nodded, but the tension between them remained, unspoken and unresolved. The knock had interrupted something that neither of them could easily forget.

As Eric shut the door and returned to the room, Della knew that their relationship had crossed a line that would change everything. The fact that he and Sylvia weren't in a loving relationship was important. Did it mean they could ethically carry on an affair? Might Sylvia even condone it, wishing for Eric to be happy?

The lines were blurry.

Eric looked ready to pick up where they left off, but Della decided to focus on the business at hand.

She cleared her throat and smoothed a few errant strands of hair that had come loose from her ponytail. "Jimmy says a profiler needs to interview you tomorrow morning."

"He told me."

"Are you flying back to Tennessee once that's done?" she asked.

"I am," he replied. "And I'd like you to go with me."

Della couldn't hide the shock on her face. "Hami, I ..."

He raised a hand to stop her. "Don't dismiss the idea before you even consider it. I doubt it would be hard for you to convince the Bureau that you should take the lead on this case. At least, until Laurel gets moved and is ready to return to work. That gives us a few days together—maybe a week, if we're lucky."

The topic of Laurel was awkward. Eric had dated her after breaking up with Della. It was something that would probably need to be discussed, at some point, especially if they would all be in close proximity in Appleman's Gap.

Della pushed that out of her mind, focusing instead on the fact that Eric had said he wanted to spend more time with her. Was sneaking around all she could expect, though?

Her mom would tell her she deserved better. She'd be right.

Della took a deep breath, trying to calm the fluttering in her chest as Eric's words sank in. She knew he wasn't just talking about working together on the case. He was asking for more. The old feelings she had tried to bury resurfaced, stronger than ever, leaving her torn between her sense of duty and her longing for something she hadn't felt in years.

Maybe they could have a future together. She hated to think that way, but he had a child now. That was what he'd wanted. Maybe with that out of the way, she could finally be enough for him.

She looked at Eric, his earnest expression tugging at her heart. He was offering her a chance to rekindle what they had lost, but at what cost? Della knew the situation was complicated, more so than it had ever been before. They weren't just two people who had drifted apart and found their way back to each other. Eric was married, even if that marriage was more for show than substance.

Her mind raced as she considered his proposal. Going to Tennessee with him, even under the guise of professional necessity, would blur the lines even further. But the pull she felt toward him was undeniable. The way he looked at her, the way he spoke to her—there was a connection that had never fully faded, and it was tempting to explore it again.

Was she ready to be the other woman? Could she live

with the guilt of sneaking around, knowing that Sylvia, regardless of the state of their marriage, was still in the picture?

Della had always prided herself on her integrity and her ability to do what was right even when it was difficult. Now, with Eric so close, asking her to take a leap with him, she found herself questioning everything.

"Hami," she began, her voice trembling slightly, "this ... us ... it's not simple. I need to know where your head is at. What are you really asking for here?"

He sighed, running a hand through his hair, clearly struggling to articulate his thoughts. "I don't want to put you in a difficult position. The truth is, though, I've missed you. I've missed what we had. I'm not happy with Sylvia, and I haven't been for a long time. We're together out of convenience, not love. I don't know what the future holds, but I do know that I want you in my life, in whatever capacity you're willing to be. Is that so wrong?"

His words were both comforting and unsettling. She could see the sincerity in his eyes, but she also saw the potential for hurt, for things to spiral out of control. Della wanted to be with Eric, but not at the expense of her own self-respect or the well-being of others.

"I care about you," she said softly, "more than I probably should. But I need to be sure that this is something we both want, for the right reasons. I can't be just an escape for you, or a way to fill a void."

He reached for her hand, his touch warm and familiar. "You're not just an escape, D. You never were. I've thought about you every day since we broke up. I didn't realize how much I needed you until you walked back into my life."

Della knew she couldn't make a decision based solely on emotions. She needed to think this through. "We have to be careful," she whispered, her voice barely audible. "If we go down this road, it could change everything. For both of us."

"I know," he said, his voice just as soft. "I'm willing to take that risk if you are."

Della didn't respond right away. Instead, she let the silence between them stretch out. She needed time to process, to weigh the risks and rewards.

"Would you be saying that on another night, when your son hadn't been kidnapped? Emotions are running high. Understandably so."

"I think I would. It isn't about that. At least, not *only* about that."

Finally, she nodded, more to herself than to him. "Let's take it one step at a time. We'll go to Tennessee. Assuming the Bureau is on board, I'll work on the case. And we'll see where things go from there. No promises. No expectations."

Eric smiled. "That's all I'm asking for. A chance."

Della knew this was dangerous territory, but as Eric squeezed her hand, she couldn't resist exploring the possibilities. Maybe, just maybe, they could find their way back to each other. If nothing else, she could help bring his son home. She would keep her guard up, knowing that the path ahead was fraught with complications.

Nine

WHEN LAUREL and Mikey arrived at Della's condo, no one was home. The lights were off, and the place was eerily quiet. Laurel felt a pang of unease settle in her chest as she used the familiar code to unlock the door and step inside. Mikey followed close behind, his eyes scanning the darkened interior.

"Do you think she's okay?" Mikey asked. He wasn't the type to jump to conclusions, but Laurel could tell he was concerned.

She hesitated before answering. "I'm not sure. She's probably just out, maybe grabbing some food or taking a walk to clear her head. But I have this feeling ..."

She trailed off, not wanting to voice her alarm just yet. Della had been someone Laurel could count on, a strong presence in her life. But lately, with everything happening, she couldn't shake the feeling that something was off. It was a nagging sensation, like an itch she couldn't quite scratch.

"Trust your gut, Sis," Mikey said. "I do."

Laurel nodded. "Yeah, Della usually texts if she's going

to be late, so that someone knows where she is. It's what single women do. I used to do the same thing, before I met Brad."

"Does she still text you, though? Since you've been back home in Tennessee?" Mikey asked.

"Usually, but not always," Laurel said. "Sometimes she texts her mom in San Antonio. Maybe I should call Paloma to see if she's heard from her daughter."

"It's getting late. Would she answer the call?"

"I don't know. Let's look around first."

Mikey shrugged, but Laurel could see the same worry reflected in his eyes. They'd been close to Della for years, and this behavior was unusual. She wasn't one to disappear without a word, especially not in the middle of everything that was happening.

"Maybe she needed some space," Mikey suggested, trying to be optimistic. "It's been a rough day."

Laurel walked over to the kitchen, noting the neatness of the counters. There were no dishes in the sink. No signs of a late-night snack or a hurried departure. Everything was in its place, just as Della liked it. Something still felt off.

"Her phone, purse, and keys are gone," Laurel noted, glancing toward the small table near the entrance where Della usually left her things. "So, she took them with her. But where would she go this late?"

Mikey frowned, moving to stand beside her. "I don't know, but I have this odd hunch ... like something's not right. And unlike you, I don't usually get hunches."

Laurel couldn't shake that feeling either. Della had been acting more distant than usual. Laurel had noticed the change, but she hadn't pressed, figuring her friend would open up when she was ready. Now she wondered if she should have pushed harder.

"I think the obvious first step is to try calling her," Mikey suggested.

"Agreed."

Laurel nodded, pulling out her phone and dialing Della's number. It rang twice before going to voicemail. She left a brief message, trying to keep the worry out of her voice. "Hey, Della. It's Laurel. Mikey and I are at your place. Just wanted to check in. Give me a call when you get this, okay?"

She ended the call and sighed, her unease growing. "I don't like this, Mikey. She's never just gone like this."

Mikey nodded, glancing out the window as if expecting to see Della walking up the sidewalk. "Should we go look for her?"

Laurel hesitated. She didn't want to overreact, but something about the situation gnawed at her. "Maybe ... or maybe we should wait a little longer. If she's out clearing her head, she'll probably be back soon."

Mikey looked at her, concern etched on his face. "Yeah, but what if something's wrong? What if she needs help?"

Laurel bit her lip, torn between staying put and trying to find Della. Just then, her phone buzzed with a message. She checked the screen, her heart skipping a beat when she saw it was from Della.

Hey, sorry I missed you. Just out for a bit.
I'll be back soon. Don't worry.

Laurel read the message aloud to her brother, feeling a mix of relief and lingering unease. "She says she'll be back soon."

He nodded, though he didn't look entirely convinced either. "Okay, that's good, I guess."

Laurel slipped her phone back into her pocket, still unsettled. Something about the message didn't sit right with her, but she couldn't put her finger on it. Della was a private person, and maybe she just needed some time alone. But then again, Della had never been one to leave her friends hanging.

"Let's wait a bit," Laurel said finally. "If she's not back in an hour, we'll call her again. Maybe start looking."

Mikey agreed, and they settled in on the couch, turning on the TV to pass the time. Laurel's mind was elsewhere, though. She couldn't shake the feeling that Della was hiding something important. She wondered if it had anything to do with Eric Hampton and his missing son. But what?

After what felt like an eternity, the door finally opened, and Della walked in, looking a little flustered. Laurel and Mikey both stood.

"Hey," Laurel said. "I hope you don't mind ... We waited."

"Hey," Della replied, offering a small smile. "Sorry about that. I just needed some air."

Laurel studied her friend, noting her disheveled appearance. Her hair was a little mussed, and there was a faint flush on her cheeks. She was in gym clothes, so maybe that explained it. Or maybe not.

"Are you okay?" Laurel asked.

Della nodded quickly, though Laurel could tell it wasn't the whole truth. "Yeah, just needed to clear my head. It's been a lot today."

Laurel exchanged a glance with her brother, who looked equally unconvinced, but neither of them pressed further.

"We were worried," Mikey said, his tone gentle. "Gotta look out for you. You know how it is. You're one of ours, even if you aren't officially a Dane sibling."

Della's smile faltered slightly. "I'm sorry. I didn't mean to make you worry. I needed to be alone for a bit."

Laurel nodded slowly, still feeling that something was off but deciding to let it go for now. "Okay. We're here if you want to talk."

Della's smile returned, though it still didn't reach her eyes. "Thanks, but I think we all need some sleep. You have a long drive tomorrow, and I suspect I'll be flying to Tennessee to join in the investigation. I'm just waiting on approval from Headquarters. Eric said I could catch a ride on his plane."

"Oh," Laurel said, her simple response worth a hundred words. She and Della didn't need to hash out the specifics or revisit the past. Besides, there'd be time for that at home in Tennessee, when they were rested.

They all agreed to call it a night, though Laurel's mind was still racing. Back at the hotel, as she got ready for bed, she couldn't shake the feeling that something was brewing beneath the surface. Something Della wasn't ready to share.

The next morning, Laurel woke up to the sound of her phone buzzing with weather alerts, plus a text from her mom making sure she'd seen the weather forecast. Severe storms were predicted for Middle Tennessee, with the possibility of tornadoes. She sighed, knowing that this was the last thing they needed.

Tornadoes were relatively common this time of year in Tennessee. Spring brought warm, moist air from the Gulf of Mexico, which collided with cooler, dry air from the north, creating the perfect conditions for severe thunderstorms and tornadoes. The landscape, with its rolling hills and valleys, could funnel winds into powerful storms that formed quickly and unpredictably. Laurel had grown up with the knowledge that these storms could strike at any moment, turning a peaceful day into one filled with chaos and destruction.

Tornado watches and warnings were a familiar part of life in Middle Tennessee, but that didn't make them any less frightening.

As they packed up the last of their luggage and loaded the vehicles, Mikey checked his phone, frowning at the latest updates. "Looks like we're in for rough weather. Tornado watches are already in effect. Mom's relaying all the information, as if we can't read it for ourselves."

They knew Maureen cared, but she could become overbearing when she thought her children might be in harm's way.

Laurel glanced at the sky, her worry deepening. "We'll just have to be careful. If things get too bad, we'll pull over. Hopefully, our weather will be okay along the drive. At least, until we get closer to home."

Brad, who was behind the wheel of the moving truck, nodded. "We'll keep an eye on it. Hopefully, we can get home before it hits."

"I just hope Eric and Della get there safely, too. I'd hate to see a storm complicate the Hampton family's situation any further," Laurel added.

"Are they flying together?" Brad asked, raising an eyebrow.

"So I hear," Laurel replied.

Deciding to leave it at that, she climbed into the passenger seat of the moving truck while Mikey, Maggie, Hazel, and Ryan piled into a car they'd rented for the journey home.

Laurel had thought she might be a blubbering mess when it came time to actually drive away from Washington, D.C., but the weather alerts worked to distract her. As they headed east on I-66, she was more focused on what they were facing than on what she was leaving behind.

Brad eyed her, making sure she was okay. "Feeling all right about the move?" he asked.

"Surprisingly, yes," she said. "I think I'm ready. Last night helped. Thank you for your thoughtfulness, my love. It was a night I'll never forget."

"Anything for you, babe," he replied.

As the day wore on and they drove southwest, the sky grew darker and the wind picked up. They kept the radio tuned to weather updates, each new report heightening the sense of urgency.

"You think it'll really be that bad?" Brad asked.

It was his first spring season living in Appleman's Gap. He'd visited then and had heard the dramatic stories about storms in the past, but this was the first year he'd have to handle the risk as Chief of Police.

Laurel shrugged. "It can get bad. It's hard to know. That's the thing about tornados—they can sneak up on you. You don't realize you're in danger until you hear that freight-train sound and the thing is right there, at your doorstep. The worst is when it comes at night."

"That sounds terrifying," Brad replied.

"I assume you have someone in the department keeping track of the weather, right?" she asked.

"Dispatch monitors it."

"So, Officer Cedric Martin will have another chance to shine, huh?" Laurel asked.

Cedric had been the dispatcher who'd answered her call last fall when she'd been kidnapped. She'd called 9-1-1 from the trunk of her car, and he'd answered. His calm, cool demeanor had helped Laurel keep a level head during a scary situation.

"He's one of our best," Brad confirmed. "He'll be at his desk, ready to assist the citizens of Appleman's Gap, should they need it."

"Good," Laurel said, placing a hand on her belly.

She wasn't generally afraid of storms, but she had to admit that everything seemed more worrisome with a growing pregnancy to protect.

Noticing the gesture, Brad placed a hand over top of hers. "We'll be okay," he said.

She nodded appreciatively.

As they neared Appleman's Gap, Laurel's phone buzzed again, this time with a tornado warning for their area. Her heart sank as she read the alert aloud. "Tornado warning for Appleman's Gap. We need to get home fast. Let's hope we can beat the storm."

PART TWO

Around and Around

Ten

"I'M PACKED," Della said when Eric opened the door of his hotel room. A fat black suitcase sat upright beside her. "The powers that be ok'ed me running point on your son's investigation. If you'll still have me, I'll fly to Tennessee with you today."

"I'm glad to hear it," Eric said, relief flooding his features as he stepped aside to let her in.

Della followed him into the room, her arm brushing his as she walked by. He smelled good. "I suspect things are about to get complicated. I'll need your help, too. Between your personal stakes and the eyes of the media on us, we have to work carefully."

"Agreed. This is a critical time," Eric replied, running a hand through his hair. "But you need to know—if we're going to do this together, we need to keep it strictly professional while we're on the job or in front of prying eyes."

"You think I don't know that?" Della asked. "I didn't come here for anything else. Billy is our priority. Let's focus on him."

"Right," he said, forcing his shoulders back and trying to rid himself of the lingering personal feelings. "I need to head to Headquarters first for that meeting with a profiler, then I have to stop by my condo to pack some things. I assume you'll want to join me? To check in at the Hoover Building and see what leads have come up?"

Della nodded. "Did you think of calling Sylvia before we leave?" she pressed, her voice softening. "She deserves to know what's happening, and she's going to be worried sick."

Eric sighed, looking away. "I know, but what do I say? She told me last night that she blames me for this. I can't keep putting her through hell."

"Or maybe she'll be grateful to hear from you," Della suggested gently. "The longer you wait, the more paranoid she will become."

"Maybe," Eric said, but his voice was flat.

Della turned on her phone, scrolling through the weather alerts as they prepared to leave. The impending storms loomed ominously on the radar. "We definitely need to move fast, before the weather gets worse. They're expecting severe storms and possible tornadoes in Middle Tennessee."

"Great. Just what we need—additional chaos to complicate matters," he muttered, raking a hand through his hair again. "But we can't let it stop us. Billy needs us."

Della nodded, feeling her heart race at the thought of the little boy in danger. "Let's get going, then."

As they made their way out of the hotel, a gust of wind rattled the oak trees lining the sidewalk, an eerie reminder of the storm brewing on the horizon, even though it was hundreds of miles away. Della felt a twinge of foreboding. It was remarkable how nature had a way of echoing their emotional turmoil.

"Do you think we'll hit bad weather even before we get to Tennessee?" she asked as they climbed into her car and drove toward Headquarters. "It always makes me nervous to fly through storms."

"Hard to say," Eric replied. "My pilots are good, but if worst comes to worst, we can always make an emergency landing."

She nodded, her expression solemn. "Billy's safety is what matters most."

Eric agreed. "I can't shake the feeling that this storm is more than just bad weather. It's almost like it's mirroring the upheaval in my life right now."

Della reached over, squeezing his hand briefly before letting go. "You're right, but we can't let it distract us. Let's get this interview done and get in the air. It should be quick. Jimmy knows you're in a hurry to get home to Tennessee."

They arrived at F.B.I. Headquarters just in time for Eric's appointment with the profiler, but the atmosphere inside was charged with an urgency that made every second feel critical. Della could sense that everyone was on edge. The stakes were high.

"Stay close," she whispered as they entered the building. Eric nodded, his jaw clenched.

They were escorted to a conference room, where the profiler, a sharp-eyed woman named Agent Lillian Harper, awaited them. "Senator Hampton, Agent Brady," she said, extending her hand. "Thank you for coming on such short notice."

"Let's get to it," Eric said, his voice resolute.

Della admired his strength.

Agent Harper opened the case file and flipped through some pages, her brow furrowing in concentration. "I know this is difficult, but we need as much information as you can give us about Billy's routine, any potential enemies, or anything unusual you may have noticed leading up to the abduction."

As Eric spoke, Della could see the pain in his eyes, the memories of his vibrant son he was desperately trying to recall just beneath the surface. She knew this was tormenting him.

"We—he plays outside most afternoons," Eric replied, his voice thick with emotion. "I usually try to be there with him when I'm in town, but I was here in D.C. that day and thought Sylvia was keeping an eye on him. I can't help but feel like I didn't do enough. I should have been at home."

"Stop that train of thought," Della urged subtly, squeezing his arm again. "This isn't your fault. We're going to bring him home. Focus on the details we need."

She noticed Agent Harper staring at her, so she added, "Senator Hampton and I are old friends."

"Right," Eric said, rubbing a hand over his face. "Billy's friends come over a lot of days, and we like to keep things calm and safe for him. Honestly, I was more concerned about his safety than anything, given the recent kidnappings." His voice shattered as he spoke the last words.

Agent Harper flipped through more pages, taking notes. "Any suspicious interactions? Anyone visiting or talking to your family recently that felt out of place?"

"Not really. We keep to our circle. We're friendly with our neighbors, but lately, we've been cautious due to everything going on in Appleman's Gap."

Della saw Eric's eyes darken with concern. The F.B.I. and local police had been working tirelessly on bringing The Cradler to justice, but the reality of the threats lingering over the town made it difficult for anyone to feel at ease.

"Has anyone approached you for favors or help that seemed unusual?" Agent Harper pressed, fixing her gaze back on Eric.

Eric shook his head but then hesitated. "There was one time, a couple of weeks ago, a man showed up at our front door. Completely unannounced. Said he was working in the area and wanted to talk about community initiatives. It felt odd. I brushed it off as a sales pitch at the time but ..." His voice trailed off, as if he were suddenly remembering details he'd overlooked before.

"What did he look like?" Della encouraged gently, wanting to pull more information from him.

"Mid-thirties, darker hair, scruffy. He was wearing a baseball cap, so I didn't see his face clearly. I thought it was harmless. He just rambled about revitalizing community parks. Looking back, though, he gave me a bad vibe. I should have told Sylvia or called someone."

"That's good intel," Harper said, taking notes rapidly. "Any idea if he's from around there? Any specific familiarity with your home or your family?"

Eric frowned, trying to summon memories. "No, he didn't say. Just mentioned wanting to improve the town, like he knew all the ins and outs. I thought he was one of those guys who just wanted to sound important. We get them sometimes in politics, trying to impress me."

Della leaned in closer. "If he had that demeanor, he may not be what he appeared," she suggested.

"Great idea," Eric agreed, nodding slowly. "I can reach out to friends and neighbors as soon as I get home. We need to be proactive."

Agent Harper scribbled down notes as they continued discussing potential leads, but Della could tell Eric was distracted. She wished she could take him into her arms and comfort him, but she knew that was silly. It struck her that the forbidden nature of doing such a thing might be why it seemed so appealing.

The questioning continued for a while longer, and Della made sure to stay focused on the matter at hand, guiding Eric through his recollections. She noted that even as the topic became more serious, they both seemed to find solace in the familiar rhythm of being together. The invisible thread of their past bound them closer with each shared tidbit of information.

Finally, the session wrapped, and they all sat back.

"I think we've gathered enough information to start running down leads," Agent Harper concluded, her voice firm and decisive. "I'll get this circulated among our task force and local law enforcement immediately. Senator Hampton, I'll be in touch if anything develops."

"Have I been completely cleared as a suspect?" he asked.

Agent Harper hesitated. "You're cleared for now. You may conduct normal activities."

"Thank you for your time and attention," he replied, his tone filled with deep gratitude. He stood and shook hands with Harper, then when she left the room he turned to Della, his expression softening. "I truly appreciate you being here for me. This experience is more difficult than I anticipated."

"It's what I'm here for, Hami," Della said, her skin tingling from the way he was looking at her.

Just then, her phone buzzed again with an incoming text. She glanced down, and read Laurel's name. It was a warning about the weather, with Laurel's opinion that it was serious.

Looking back at Eric, Della sensed the emotional storm brewing there. "The weather alerts sound troubling," Della admitted. "But let's focus on Billy right now. Once we land, we'll make a plan on what to do next."

"Okay."

Once they picked up some things from his condo, the drive to the airport was short. Della stole glances at Eric, both comforted and unsettled by his presence. She could feel the familiar electricity between them.

As she pulled into the airport parking lot, Della found herself grappling with her emotions. The airport was bustling, filled with travelers darting around and families hugging goodbye. Della wished she could be part of that normalcy instead of being tangled in this web of uncertainty and pain.

"You ready?" she asked softly, turning off the engine.

Eric took a deep breath and nodded. "I guess we're about to find out the kind of luck we have today."

Despite the uncertainty ahead, Della couldn't stop thinking about the connection they'd reignited. Could they truly keep things professional? The closeness their shared past fostered was one that could easily become blurred, shifting dangerously from camaraderie back to something intimate. She didn't want to lose any of the progress she could make on the case. Yet still, the potential for a deeper personal relationship existed. Eric seemed willing to pursue something more.

They stepped out of the car and walked toward the terminal. Eric held the door open for Della as they entered the bustling airport and made their way to the hangar where his private jet sat waiting.

Della found herself exchanging glances with Eric often. Each time their eyes met, there was an unspoken understanding. She could see the weight on his shoulders and the anguish rippling beneath the surface. It fueled her determination to see this through.

"We should come up with a plan for as soon as we land," Della suggested as they boarded the plane and took their seats. "We can't let any time slip away."

"Absolutely," Eric agreed. "I'll need to reach out to law enforcement in Appleman's Gap to coordinate with them as soon as we arrive. With the storm predicted, they might have to adjust their strategies on the ground. I want to ensure every resource is on alert. I want to offer my support to their efforts."

Della nodded. "Brad Tate is Chief of Police now." She waited to see if he'd recognize the name, but he didn't seem to. "Laurel's fiancé."

"Oh." He hesitated, then added, "That shouldn't be a problem."

Eleven

NO ONE WOULD HAVE BLAMED Laurel if she'd gone right home to bed. Her ankles were swollen, her bladder was terribly uncomfortable, and she was sore from riding in the moving truck that had less than luxurious seats. Pregnancy wasn't the ideal time for travel. It was too late to unload today, anyway.

Dedicated as she was, though, she insisted on getting down to the station to meet with Agents Samira Aziz and Malik Washington to discuss Billy's case.

Laurel moved quickly through the lobby, mindful of the impending storm, her resolve stronger than the exhaustion tugging at her eyelids. The flickering lights above and the distant rumble of thunder reminded her that time was of the essence. Billy needed her.

She quickly made her way to the conference room, where Samira and Malik were already deep in conversation, poring over the latest reports and witness statements. The dim light from the overhead lamps reflected off the polished conference table, casting their faces in sharp relief. They looked up as she entered, their expressions shifting.

"Agent Dane!" Samira said, relief flooding her voice as she got up to greet Laurel. "We didn't expect you so soon. I thought you'd need more time to settle in after the move."

"I know the timing isn't ideal," Laurel replied, shaking her head as she slid into an empty chair, "but I couldn't just sit at home while we have a child out there who needs us."

Malik nodded in agreement. "You're right. And you bring a perspective we could really use. Given your history, you might see connections that we missed."

Laurel bristled at the reference to her own kidnapping as a child, but she shrugged it off. "What do you have so far?"

"We've interviewed Sylvia," Samira began, flipping through her notes. "She's distraught, understandably, but very cooperative. She provided us a timeline of the day Billy went missing and a list of individuals who visited their home recently."

"Anyone stand out?" Laurel asked, her instincts kicking in as she leaned forward in her seat.

"Just one man," Malik said, eyebrows knitting together as he spoke. "Senator Hampton mentioned a strange visitor a couple of weeks prior. The description sounds familiar to someone we found on security footage near the Hampton residence on the day of the abduction. We're still working on putting the puzzle pieces together."

"Do we have an ID?"

"Not yet."

"What did he look like?" Laurel asked, already mentally organizing a list of suspects.

"Mid-thirties, dark hair, and scruffy." Samira's voice

trailed off as she moved to a whiteboard and began jotting down the details. "Baseball cap, and he seemed overly interested in their family's activities."

Laurel felt a knot tighten in her stomach. "Could he have had ulterior motives? This could be connected to the recent kidnappings in Appleman's Gap."

"Possibly," Malik said.

"Or he could have been a harmless passerby," Samira added. "Given everything that's happened, we can't afford to take any chances. We need to dig deeper."

Laurel glanced at the window. It was dark outside, but the bright moon shone on ominous clouds that were rolling in, threatening to break. "What's our next step?"

"Surveillance footage from the neighborhood is our best bet," Malik responded. "We'll check for anything that matches the description or activities of this man."

"Let's also see if there's any connection to known suspects or recent parolees in the area with that description," Laurel suggested.

"Of course," Samira said as her pen moved rapidly across the whiteboard. "We should also maintain communication with Senator Hampton. He needs to know what's going on. He was scheduled to fly here with Agent Brady today, but we haven't heard from either of them yet. I assume they'll reach out tomorrow morning."

"Agreed," Laurel said, her heart aching for Eric's family.

She remembered the despair in his eyes when the commotion took hold at the Cherry Blossom Festival. This was about more than just a case. It was about a father's love for his son—and a child's need for safety. The fact that Laurel had dated

Eric only made her more motivated to help bring his son home.

"Let's get to work then," Malik said, pushing his chair back as he rose. "We'll split up to cover more ground. Samira and I can talk to local cops and look through police records. You can start with the surveillance footage. Sound good?"

Laurel nodded, feeling the urgency. "I'll look through the video and see if I can find anything before the storm hits."

The three of them got up and moved with purpose. The building felt charged with energy, even as the wind outside started to howl.

As Laurel began her search for the security footage from the surrounding neighborhood, she couldn't help but glance at her phone. There were several missed messages from her parents and siblings, asking if she was okay amid the flood warnings and weather alerts. There was a flurry of communication as everyone got settled in a safe place and hunkered down. They had dropped Mikey off at his house in Knoxville on the way home, but Maggie, Hazel, and Ryan were all just arriving in Appleman's Gap after the long trip.

Brad had dropped Laurel off at the station, then gone to retrieve Lilly from Maureen's house. Laurel and Brad were both eager to see the pup. They hoped Mack had taken good care of her. Laurel had at least an hour before they'd return, and she intended to make the most of it.

Taking a deep breath, she texted everyone back quickly.

> I'm at the station. We're working on finding Billy. Please stay safe and keep an eye on the weather updates! I'll get home soon.

The response buzzed back immediately from Hazel.

Laurel blinked back tears, feeling a swell of appreciation for her family. They always knew how to lift her spirit, even amidst the chaos.

A few minutes later, she made her way to the back room housing the surveillance footage. She settled into the chair and booted up the system.

Working quickly, she navigated through the interface to access footage from the Hampton neighborhood. Her pulse quickened as she began filtering the hours leading up to Billy's disappearance. The screen flickered to life, displaying grainy images of the street—children playing, parents chatting, and occasional cars passing by. Amidst the mundane moments, Laurel's gaze sharpened, focused on every detail of the clips being pulled up.

As minutes turned into what felt like hours, frustration began to creep in. A handful of potential suspects appeared, but none matched the description provided. She sighed, rubbing the back of her neck, trying to alleviate the tension. Time was ticking, and she could feel the storm closing in on their plans.

Just then, something caught her attention.

A man—a silhouette with dark hair—crossed the screen, walking briskly past the Hampton residence. Laurel's instincts flared to life as she noted the figure's baseball cap, pulling it low over his face. It was a brief moment, barely three seconds long, but it was enough to get her attention. She rewound the footage, watching the man again and again, searching for anything that could set off alarm bells.

"Come on," she whispered to herself, desperate for clarity. "Show me more."

Her fingertip hovered above the play button as she stopped at that moment, ready to capture a screenshot. The image froze, highlighting the figure's posture, the way he seemed to check over his shoulder, darting nervous glances—just as Eric had described.

There was something about this man that didn't sit right with her. Not to mention, she was beginning to hear Bach's Cello Suite No. 1 in G Major in her mind. Laurel didn't always hear classical music when she was onto something, but when she did, she knew to trust it. The cue had never failed her. Not once.

"Gotcha," she said softly, heart thudding as she saved the frame.

A buzzing sound brought her focus back. Her phone vibrated on the desk, and she glanced down to see a text from Brad.

> On my way back. Minor storm delay at the grocery store while getting snacks for your storm watch. The place was mobbed.

Laurel smiled, gratitude filling her heart. "Always looking out," she murmured to herself. She quickly shot him a reply.

> Thanks! See you at the station when you get here. Collected some potential intel on a suspect.

When she returned her gaze to the security footage, the storm suddenly intensified outside, a flash of lightning illuminating the entire room. She pressed on, determined, as the wind picked up.

With the storm brewing outside, Laurel felt a renewed surge of determination. She couldn't afford to be intimidated by the elements when a child's life hung in the balance. The shadowy figure she had captured remained frozen on the screen, a haunting reminder of the seriousness of the situation.

Staring intently at the image, Laurel knew she needed more information. She quickly saved the frame and jotted down notes on what she'd observed. The details were hazy, but she needed to share this with Samira and Malik as soon as possible.

"Focus, Laurel," she whispered to herself, shaking off distractions as she continued to scour the footage.

The minutes dragged on. Outside, the storm grew fiercer, hammering rain against the windows as the thunder cracked overhead.

Suddenly, she noticed another spot of movement in the corner of the screen. Squinting closer, she leaned forward, her excitement building as the classical music in her head continued. It was another figure, this one dressed in a darker jacket. He seemed to linger near the Hampton home, casually glancing toward their yard. By the time he left the frame, she noted the time stamp beside the video, recognizing that this was moments before Billy had been reported missing.

"Who are you?" she murmured, tagging this still image next to the first.

Realizing she needed to get this information out quickly, Laurel snapped a couple of pictures with her phone. She swiped to change screens and send a message to Samira and

Malik just as the room shook with a rumble of loud thunder. The lights flickered, then went out, plunging her into darkness.

Had she hit save on the computer? She hoped so.

"Great," she muttered, fumbling for her phone to use its flashlight feature. As the little beam illuminated the room, other emergency lights flickered on, though they provided nothing more than a dull glow.

"Seriously?" she whispered, half-amused, half-annoyed at the inconvenience. A part of her knew that this was typical of any significant storm in Tennessee. The power outages were frustrating, but they wouldn't slow her down.

Laurel retraced her steps and gathered herself, resolving to ride out the storm and remain focused on her priority. She hoped her family was safe as she glanced at her phone again, willing it to light up with responses.

Nothing.

She took a deep breath, trying to calm the apprehension swelling in her chest. The storm was fierce. She could hear the roar of the wind, which was getting louder and more ferocious all the time. The lights flickered again, momentarily illuminating fragile shadows dancing along the walls.

Through it all, though, she kept her instincts sharp. With each flash of lightning, she was reminded that she had a job to do. The urgency in her gut was a steady drum, pushing her to stay vigilant. She used the low light of her phone to scan the room, checking to make sure nothing essential had been left behind.

The sounds of the storm grew louder, and just then, her phone vibrated unexpectedly. Laurel quickly held the device up to her face, and relief washed over her when she saw that Malik was texting her.

> We just talked to the neighbors. No one saw anything unusual when Billy was taken, but someone caught a glimpse of a man acting suspiciously last night.

Laurel's heart raced as she typed back.

> I have something, too. I found footage of a man lurking around the Hampton home right before Billy went missing. He matches Eric's description. He's a possible suspect.

Before she could click send, another image flickered in her mind's eye—the darker figure she'd seen on the security footage. It was an eerie reminder that this might not be as simple as it seemed. Whatever gripped Appleman's Gap had a monstrous face hiding in the shadows.

Malik's reply came back almost immediately.

> We're returning to the station now. Are you still there? Can you meet us in the conference room?

> Of course.

Laurel texted back quickly, gathering her essentials. The faint emergency lights cast a muted glow as she rose from her chair, steadying herself against the table.

Suddenly, the darkness around her felt uncomfortable. Something bad was coming.

Navigating the dim corridors of the station, she tried to focus on the task ahead, keeping her breaths even. Della, Eric, and Billy needed her strength.

DELLA TAPPED her fingers against the kitchen counter at her rental home in downtown Appleman's Gap. Eric sat at the nearby table, his head in his hands.

They'd landed at the tiny air field hours ago, then had taken a rental car to the rental house. They had gotten one of the last cars available. As it turned out, the same home that Della had stayed in previously was available. It was nice—a brick bungalow with a swing on the front porch and a garden out back. She felt comfortable here. Except that it was time for Eric to go home, and he was dragging his feet.

"The winds are picking up out there," she said as she eyed him suspiciously. "You had better get home to Sylvia before the worst of it arrives."

He stood suddenly, closing the distance between them and leaning dangerously close. Della could smell his familiar scent, and it made her pulse quicken.

"I don't want to go home," he said. "I want to stay here. With you."

Her breath hitched. "Hami, this is not the right time. You

need to focus on Billy and your family. Whatever's happening between us, it can wait until this storm passes."

He stepped back, clearly frustrated, running a hand through his hair. "I can't think about anything but you right now. I want to help find my son, but I also can't shake you from my mind. You're the only one that feels like home to me. I don't care where we are or where we go. *You* feel like home."

Della's heart pounded, and for a moment, she toyed with the idea of giving in. With the storm brewing outside and the missing boy hanging like a weight over their heads, surrendering to the moment felt reckless.

"This isn't just about us," she said.

"I know that," he replied, his voice low and intense. "But everything feels so uncertain. I want you by my side as I face this. If we're going to do this right, I need you with me—beyond just the investigation. I can't help it. I care about you, D."

And there it was again, the pull between their shared past and uncertain future. Della found herself grappling with her longing, fighting the instincts warring inside her.

"We have to focus," she reiterated gently, though her resolve was weakening. "You have your family to consider. They need you more than I do right now."

"Do they?" Eric challenged, the edge of his voice sharp. "Is that why I was informed about my son's abduction by the media instead of my wife? She hasn't contacted me since we spoke last night."

"I—" Della froze, taken aback by the raw honesty of his words. "It's not fair to take your pain out on me. You know I'm not the enemy."

"I know," he sighed, his shoulders sagging as he dropped into a nearby chair. "It just feels like everything is crumbling. I let my family down, and Billy is missing. I can't keep pretending it doesn't hurt."

"I get it."

"You remember how Laurel said to tell me she was sorry?" he asked. "Well, she's sorry for getting mad when we broke up and telling me she wished me bad luck in love and life. Right now, it kind of feels like I'm cursed."

Della walked over to him, her heart aching for the father who couldn't separate his emotions from the storm brewing outside and in his life. She placed a hand on his shoulder.

"We're going to find him," she said. "And when we do, we'll have a discussion about us. If you still think we could have a future."

She stepped close, and as she moved, he grabbed her around the waist and pulled her to him.

"I want you," he said as his chin grazed the bottom of her breasts, his breath husky with desire.

Della's heart raced, a mix of fear and thrill running through her veins. The ache of longing felt familiar. It was an old wound being reopened. She knew this moment could tip things in any direction. One step too far and they would plunge into uncertainty.

Although, she wondered, would that be so bad?

"We can't," she breathed, feeling the heat radiate from his body. "This isn't the time. We have to keep our heads clear."

Eric released her slightly but held her gaze, the intensity in his eyes undiminished. "I can't help what I feel. You're still the one I want to turn to when everything feels out of control. I need you to be by my side, especially now. You know it's more than just the investigation for me."

Della felt torn between the warmth of his words and the reality of their current situation. She brushed a strand of hair behind her ear, trying to distance herself from the vulnerability that was drawing them closer.

"You're frightened, and that's normal," she said. "I get it. We have to channel that energy into finding Billy, not into whatever this is between us."

"Don't you see?" Eric's voice dropped to a whisper. "Where I am doesn't feel right without you. I don't want you just to help me through this. I want you because ... because I care about you. I found myself thinking about you even before you approached me at the festival yesterday. I'd been thinking of calling you."

The sincerity in his tone tightened the space around them, and for a heartbeat, Della pondered the possibility of giving in to what had been simmering beneath the surface. The thought of Sylvia flashed in her mind. It was a reminder that while Eric might be willing to risk everything, she could not be that kind of woman.

"Let's focus on Billy first," she insisted, firming her resolve. "We owe it to him and to ourselves to stay professional."

He persisted, undeterred. He slid his big, strong hands up and under Della's shirt, grazing the sensitive skin with his fingertips. She gasped, feeling a pressure begin to build between her legs.

"If it's Sylvia you're worried about, don't. She and I have talked about seeing other people. We're nothing more than roommates, at this point. I promise," he explained. "We were in love once, but it's all for appearances now. Besides, I never loved her like I loved you."

Della closed her eyes, remembering what it felt like to hold him. To kiss him. To make love to him.

But their situation was complicated.

"It's not just Sylvia," she said, her voice strained as she struggled through temptation. "You were with Laurel for two whole years after we broke up. I don't know how I feel about that. She's one of my closest friends."

"Then we can talk about it ... over breakfast tomorrow morning. I'll cook my eggs Benedict that you always loved."

He moved his hands higher, tracing her nipples through her lacy bra, as he gently slid her petite body between his legs.

Della's breath caught in her throat, the heat between them igniting a conflict within her that threatened to boil over. "Hami, we can't," she whispered.

His gaze intensified, rich with longing and need. "Why not? We're both here right now, passionate and vulnerable. This moment is real. I don't want to pretend that we can't feel this," he said. "You feel it, D. Your body is telling me you do."

"Because we have responsibilities. We need to find Billy," she insisted. The thought of Billy, the innocent child caught in this nightmare, grounded her. "I don't want to lose sight of what's truly important."

Eric's hands stilled, but his expression didn't shift. The storm outside continued its furious assault, wind thrashing against the windows like a beast trying to break in. It mirrored the tempest within the room, a wild mixture of emotions pulled taut between them.

"I care about my son, more than anything. But I also care

about you. This connection is undeniable. Can't you see? You can't do anything with the investigation while this storm is going on, anyway. Be real." Eric's voice was raw, desperation seeping through as he pulled her even closer, eyes pleading.

The door to the hallway creaked slightly, and Della couldn't help but glance toward it, the fear of being caught mixing with the thrill of Eric's proximity. "What happens if anyone finds out? If your family finds out? What about Sylvia?"

"They're not here, and right now, all that matters is you and me," Eric shot back, his hands finding her waist again and sliding down toward her backside.

Della closed her eyes, battling against thoughts of the bigger picture. The intensity of their surroundings and the closeness of their bodies made it difficult to think.

She pulled away, creating distance between them. "Focus, Hami. We need to be strong. Now is not the time to fall into old patterns."

Solidifying his resolve, Eric stood. He pulled Della's hips against his and she could feel the length of him pressing forward. He leaned in, gently kissing her neck.

"Make love to me, D.," he said between kisses.

Della had spent years trying to forget how deeply she felt for Eric. How they were once so intertwined, emotionally and physically.

She couldn't let herself go there. Not when they were in the midst of such a chaotic situation. Not when they both had responsibilities that loomed larger than their rekindled feelings. Could she?

"Hami," she whispered, trying to keep her voice steady

despite the storm of emotions surging within her. "We can't do this. Not now. I'm sorry. Maybe another time."

Still, Eric's proximity was intoxicating. The way he held her waist and peered into her soul made it hard to resist.

"Please," he said softly, his voice barely above a whisper. "Just one night together. One night where we can forget everything else. Do you want me to call Sylvia and get her permission? I wouldn't lie about such a thing. You know that. You know *me*."

Della hesitated. The winds howled outside, rattling the window panes.

"Just one night," she found herself saying against her better judgment before she even realized the words had escaped her lips. The need in his eyes was magnetic, and suddenly, they were lost in each other, words giving way to instincts that had lain dormant for far too long.

Eric pulled her close again, their bodies meeting in a rush of warmth and urgency. He captured her lips with his, sweet and hesitant at first, but slowly deepening with the hunger that had built between them. Della gave in, allowing the kiss to envelop her wholeheartedly.

She melted against him, their bodies fitting together like a glove as they tasted the sweetness of what could have been—and perhaps, what still could be, if they dared to embrace it after the storm passed.

"Hami, I don't have a condom," she said breathlessly.

Neither wanted to voice it, but they understood. Della couldn't have children. Birth control wasn't a concern.

"Are you clean?" he asked.

Della's brow furrowed. "For STDs? Yeah, I am. Are you?"

"Yes," he nodded. "It sounds like we're okay without

using protection. Nothing we haven't done before. What? A million times?"

"Okay."

As the kiss deepened, Della felt the world outside fade away into the background, the echoes of thunder merging with the pounding of her heart. Moments stretched into an eternity, her longstanding desire for Eric igniting a fire she thought had been extinguished.

Della's fingers trembled as they gripped the fabric of Eric's shirt, pulling him closer as the passion between them ignited. The storm outside intensified further, winds howling and rain lashing against the windows, but it was nothing compared to the tempest raging within.

The familiar scent of him, the taste of his lips, and the feel of his strong hands caressing her skin were like magic. It all felt so right and so wrong at the same time.

Eric's kisses moved from her lips to her jaw, then slid down her neck, leaving a trail of heat in their wake. Della gasped as he nipped at the sensitive skin, her body responding with a surge of need that she hadn't felt in years. The logical part of her mind screamed at her to stop, to pull away before they crossed a line they couldn't uncross. The rest of her—the part that had loved Eric deeply, that had missed him fiercely—craved the connection they once had.

"Hami, we should stop," she whispered, her voice wavering with uncertainty.

But Eric's hands were already slipping under her shirt again, his touch setting her nerves on fire. He pushed the fabric up, his fingertips grazing her ribs, making her shiver with anticipation. His eyes, dark with desire, locked onto hers, pleading with her to let go completely. To give in to what they both wanted.

"I need you," he murmured against her skin, his breath hot and urgent. "I've needed you for so long."

Her resolve crumbled as his body molded to hers. Every inch of her yearned for him, for the comfort and the passion that only he could provide. The years apart melted away, and all that mattered was the man in front of her. The man who had once been her everything.

With a shaky breath, she tangled her fingers in his hair and pulled his mouth to hers, kissing him with a desperation that matched his own. His hands roamed her body, exploring the curves and contours that had changed over the years but were still so familiar to him. She moaned softly as his touch grew bolder, his lips claiming hers in a kiss that was both possessive and tender.

He moved to the kitchen and lifted her onto the counter. Her legs wrapped around his waist, pulling him closer. The friction between them was electric, sending waves of pleasure through her that made her arch against him. Eric groaned, his hands sliding down to cup her backside, lifting her just enough to press his hardness against her core.

Della's breath caught as he ground against her, the thin barrier of fabric doing nothing to dampen the intensity of the moment. Her mind spun with the implications of what they were about to do, but her body wouldn't let her pull away.

She wanted this. She wanted *him*.

Eric's hands moved to the waistband of her pants, his fingers deftly undoing the button and zipper before sliding them down her hips. Della moaned as he pushed the fabric aside, his hand slipping between her thighs to find her already wet and ready for him. She gasped, her head falling back as he teased her, his fingers brushing against her most sensitive spot with expert precision.

"Hami," she breathed, her voice trembling with need. "Please."

He didn't need any more encouragement. In one fluid motion, he freed himself from his pants and positioned himself at her entrance. Their eyes met, and for a moment, time seemed to stand still. The storm outside raged on, but inside, there was only the two of them.

With a slow, deliberate thrust, Eric entered her, filling her completely. Della cried out, the sensation overwhelming as he stretched and filled her in a way that only he could. She clung to him, her nails digging into his shoulders as he began to move, each thrust pushing her closer to the edge.

The pleasure built quickly, their bodies moving together in a rhythm that felt both familiar and new. It was as if they had never been apart. As if they had been made for this moment. Della's moans filled the air, mixing with the sound of the storm as she lost herself in the pleasure of being with him.

"D.," Eric groaned, his voice rough with desire. "I've missed this. I've missed you."

She didn't respond with words. Instead, she tightened her legs around him, urging him deeper, harder. The counter beneath her provided leverage, allowing him to thrust into her with more force, driving them both closer to release. The tension coiled tighter and tighter within her, her body tingling with the promise of climax.

"Hami, I'm—" she gasped, unable to finish the sentence

as the pleasure exploded within her, sending her spiraling into ecstasy.

Eric followed her over the edge, his body tensing as he found his release. They held onto each other as the waves of pleasure washed over them, their breathing heavy and ragged. For a moment, they just clung to each other, the aftershocks of their passion leaving them trembling.

As the storm outside began to calm, so did the storm within them. Eric gently pulled out of her, his hands caressing her as he helped her down from the counter. They stood there, wrapped in each other's arms, neither wanting to break the connection that had just been rekindled in a mighty way.

"I don't regret this," Eric whispered, pressing a soft kiss to her temple. "Not for a second."

Della sighed, resting her head against his chest. "Neither do I," she admitted, though she knew the road ahead would be complicated.

For now, though, they were together, and that was enough.

The future could wait.

Thirteen

A LOUD SOUND blared from somewhere outside, echoing within the concrete walls of the police station.

"What was that?" Samira asked, her voice strained.

Samira had only recently moved to Tennessee from Northern California. She wasn't accustomed to this kind of weather.

"Tornado siren," Laurel said. "We need to get to the basement."

As they reached the basement door, the sound of the siren grew louder, and they could hear the wind picking up outside. It was an eerie rumbling sound now, familiar to Laurel yet incredibly frightening.

"Stick together!" Malik shouted over the cacophony.

A small crowd of other officers and station employees followed. Luckily, it was late enough in the evening that the building was mostly empty. The majority of folks were, hopefully, safe at home.

Laurel wondered about Brad and Lilly.

They descended the stairs, the heavy door slamming shut

behind them, muffling the sound of the storm above. The basement was cool and dim, illuminated by emergency lights that flickered intermittently, giving the space an unsettling ambiance. Files and boxes were stacked against the walls, the remnants of old, forgotten cases.

Laurel took a deep breath. "We need to wait it out," she reassured Malik and Samira, hoping to instill some sense of calm in the situation. "We'll be okay."

"Do we have a weather radio down here?" Samira asked, rummaging through the boxes. "We should, at least, have some updates."

"I can check over by the filing cabinets," Malik suggested, moving toward a corner of the basement where old radio equipment was stored.

Laurel glanced around, noting the setup they had going. The basement of the police station was not a comfortable place, but it would have to do. She hoped Brad would walk through the door at any minute. She didn't like the idea of him out on the roads.

"Let's keep our heads clear. Stay focused on the investigation while we wait," Laurel said, trying to sound steady. "If there's a break, we'll get back to the case."

"Okay," Samira and Malik said with a nod.

They settled into their respective corners of the basement, forming a makeshift command center as they waited for more information to trickle in. The sirens continued to wail in the distance, and every so often, deep rumbles of thunder shook the walls around them.

"What if the storm takes out the backup power?" Samira said, her voice tinged with worry. "We may lose all comms with the outside."

Laurel shrugged. "The building is sturdy. Focus on staying calm and prepared to act if anything changes. We've trained for uncertain situations like this."

"Right," Malik contributed. "The storm is the least of our worries if we don't keep our heads on straight."

Just then, a loud crash echoed from above, followed by a deep rumble that rattled the floor. Laurel's stomach dropped. The sound was too close for comfort.

"Okay, everyone, stay sharp," she instructed. "Did anyone find a weather radio?"

"Found one!" an officer called from the other side of the room.

"Turn it on," Laurel said.

Unexpectedly, the emergency lights flickered once more before plunging the basement into darkness, leaving the sound of the whirling air and the distant howls of the storm above. After a few seconds, static from the radio sounded as the device came to life.

"Thank God," Malik said, his voice strained.

"I'll listen in," the officer near the radio promised.

"Thanks," Laurel said. "What's your name, sir?" She thought his voice sounded familiar.

"Sure thing, ma'am," he replied. "I'm Officer Cedric Martin."

Laurel's brows shot up. "You're the one who helped me on the 9-1-1 call last fall. Do you remember?" She rushed over, feeling the desire to hug him.

"Of course, I do," he said, sensing her feelings and offering an arm for a warm hug. His rich brown skin and strong features made him look handsome in his police uniform. A gold band sparkled from his left hand. "You did great that day. And I see that your little one is getting big." He looked at her pregnant belly admiringly.

"I couldn't have done it without you," Laurel replied. "Thank you for what you did. From both of us." She patted her belly while smiling at him appreciatively.

As nice as it was to connect and reminisce, the reality of their current situation pressed on. Cedric nodded, then turned his attention back to the weather radio.

"I'll try to find a flashlight," Malik said, fumbling through his bag. "Has anyone checked for a generator in the building? There should be something on the property."

Laurel shook her head. "Honestly? I have no idea. It's not something I'd thought to ask. Chief Tate would know, but I don't have a phone signal and can't call him. Let's just make sure we're ready to move if we need to."

Voices whispered to one another in nervous speculation. They couldn't afford to let panic set in.

Minutes passed as they fumbled through the darkness, trying to maintain a sense of normalcy and organization. Then finally, the emergency lights buzzed back to life.

"Lights are good, but hear that?" Malik said, his brow furrowing as he tilted his head. "Sounds like the wind is getting even stronger."

Laurel strained to listen, and she felt the floor vibrate slightly. "It's not just the wind," she murmured, heart racing. "I think we need to move away from the door."

With a bang, the sound of something striking the building crescendoed.

"That doesn't sound good," she said.

"What does the radio say?" Malik asked Cedric.

Cedric lowered his brow and turned the volume knob,

tuning in the static, until a clear voice broke through the noise.

"Attention! We have a confirmed tornado on the ground, approaching Appleman's Gap from the west. All citizens are to seek immediate shelter. Keep away from windows and doors.

If you are unable to evacuate, find a sturdy piece of furniture or a low-lying area to protect yourself."

Laurel felt her stomach drop. She was safe in the basement, but she desperately wanted to know that her loved ones above ground were okay. Brad should have been there by now. And Lilly.

"Has anyone checked communications?" Laurel asked as she crouched closer, leaning to speak with Samira while keeping an eye on the static-filled radio. "What do we know about what's happening up there?"

"The officers who work dispatch are down here with us," Samira said urgently. "The department can't send emergency services out in these conditions."

"Then what are all the sirens we hear?"

Samira shrugged, her silky black hair swaying. "Maybe the fire department. I'm not sure."

"Damn," Laurel muttered.

"What about vehicles?" Malik asked. "What's the status? If we need to move quickly for any reason, better to check."

Laurel nodded sympathetically. Malik was beginning to panic, and she felt bad for him. He wasn't from around here, either.

"That's a good point," she said, "but I think we're trapped, for the time being. Nothing we can do but wait until it's safe again."

Just then, the radio crackled back to life, and Cedric adjusted the volume. "The storm has intensified. If you're in or around Appleman's Gap, Tennessee, take immediate shelter. I repeat, we have confirmed a tornado on the ground in Appleman's Gap, heading east. Take immediate shelter."

The room shook violently, and the lights flickered again. Everyone held their breath.

"I've never been through anything like this," Samira whispered, her voice trembling.

"It's going to pass," Laurel reassured her. "Just a few more minutes, and the worst will be over."

The radio crackled again, the announcer's voice now barely audible over the roar of the storm. "Tornado confirmed … severe damage reported … stay in place until further notice."

Laurel's thoughts drifted to her family. She knew they were scattered across the town—Brad, her siblings, her mom and Mack, and her dad all trying to weather the storm in their own ways. Her fingers itched to grab her phone, to check in with them, but she knew it was useless. The signal was gone, and the best she could do was hope they were all safe. She closed her eyes and said a silent prayer for their safety.

A loud crash echoed through the building, followed by the sound of glass shattering somewhere above them. The noise was so close, it made everyone jump, instinctively ducking lower.

Laurel's mind raced with thoughts of what could have caused the crash. A window blown out? Something torn loose from the roof?

The basement was far from ideal as a storm shelter, but it was all they had. It was certainly better than not having a basement at all. Due to the rock present underground in much of Middle Tennessee, having a basement was a luxury. Most homes and buildings were on a crawlspace or slab with no shelter underground. Some had separate storm shelters in the yard, but even those were becoming less common.

The wind continued to howl, the sound so loud it seemed to be coming from every direction at once. Laurel crouched down, pulling Samira and Malik closer, trying to comfort them as best she could. The floor vibrated beneath them, as if the entire building was being shaken by some invisible force.

"Just hold on," Laurel murmured, more to herself than anyone else. "It'll be over soon."

The minutes stretched on, each one feeling like an eternity. Every small sound was magnified by the darkness and fear. Laurel's mind spun with worst-case scenarios. The kind she tried to keep at bay but couldn't help considering.

What if the tornado hit the station directly? What if the building couldn't withstand it? What if they became stuck under rubble without food, water, or fresh air? Or worse, what if Brad was out there in it? What if his truck wasn't strong enough to keep him from being carried away? The conventional wisdom was to get out and get in a ditch. Would he do that? It sounded completely terrifying.

Laurel placed a protective hand on her pregnant belly, praying harder that she, her child, and the rest of her family would make it through this.

Finally, after what felt like hours but was likely only minutes, the sound of the wind began to subside. The roar lessened, fading into a distant rumble. The trembling of the floor eased, and the oppressive pressure in the air lifted slightly.

Laurel released a breath she hadn't realized she'd been holding. "I think it's passing," she said, her voice hushed. "Stay put for now, but I think we're going to be okay."

The others slowly began to relax, though no one moved from their spots. The radio continued to buzz with static, but the voice on the other end was now issuing warnings for other areas east of them, confirming that the worst of the storm had moved on from Appleman's Gap.

Laurel's thoughts turned back to her family. The urge to check on them was overwhelming, but she knew they couldn't leave the basement until they were absolutely sure it was safe.

Another ten minutes passed before the radio crackled again, this time with a voice declaring the immediate threat over.

"We'll need to check the damage," Laurel said, standing up and brushing off her knees. "But let's take it slow. Make sure the way is clear."

Malik and Samira nodded, rising to their feet, relief washing over their faces. Together, they led the way back toward the stairs, cautious with each step.

The scene upstairs was one of havoc. The windows in the lobby had indeed been blown out, shards of glass scattered across the floor. Papers and debris were strewn everywhere, and the front door hung on its hinges, barely attached. Laurel's heart sank as she took it all in.

"They'll need to get a team in here to clean up," Malik said, surveying the damage. "Where is Chief Tate?"

Laurel wished she knew. More than anything, she hoped Brad was safe.

"I don't know. Let's check outside," she suggested, heading for the door. "We need to see what else is going on."

As they stepped outside, the town of Appleman's Gap came into view. The familiar scenery was completely transformed by the storm. Trees were down, blocking roads and sidewalks. Power lines lay tangled on the ground, some sparking faintly in the night. The air was thick with the smell of wet earth and the faint scent of something burning.

Laurel's phone buzzed in her pocket, startling her. She pulled it out, relieved to see that she had a signal again. Dozens of missed alerts and messages flooded in, but one caught her eye immediately—a weather warning, advising that the storm had passed but cautioning that more severe weather could follow in the coming days.

"They weren't kidding about tornado season," Malik muttered, reading over her shoulder.

Laurel nodded, already dialing Brad's number. As it rang, she glanced around at the destruction, wondering what this meant for their investigation. She hoped Billy was somewhere safe. She also wondered if Della had arrived in town with Eric yet, and she wondered how they'd fared in the storm.

When Brad answered, his voice was calm but concerned. "Babe, you okay? The storm hit hard here."

"We're fine," she assured him, "but it looks bad. The station took some damage, and the town ..." She trailed off, her gaze sweeping over the battered landscape.

"Same here," Brad said. "Your parents' place took a hit, but everyone is all right. The real problem is the roads. They're blocked all over the place. I might not be able to get out of here tonight. At least, not in my truck. I really need to get to the station, too. What kind of Chief would I be if I don't come right in to organize a response?"

"You went back to Mom and Dad's?"

"I didn't have much choice," Brad said. "When I got out of the grocery store, it was obvious that Lilly and I needed to take shelter right then. Your parents' house was right around the corner, so I went back. I tried to call you, but no signal."

"I'm just glad you're safe. Is everyone else okay?" she asked.

"Yes, everyone is fine," Brad replied. "Lilly and Sully, too. Now that I know you and the baby are good, my concern is getting to you. What are we going to do?"

Laurel sighed, glancing up at the swirling clouds still hanging ominously overhead. "Let's play it by ear. If you can't get here, I think I can get home ... or to you at Mom and Dad's house. I can ask someone to drive me. Most of the cars in the parking lot look okay. If it's too risky, though, I'll stay put. I see some downed power lines."

"Agreed," Brad replied. "Be safe. Stay in touch. I love you, babe. It's going to be okay."

As she ended the call, Laurel frowned. The storm was just one more complication in a situation that was already spiraling out of control. As much as she wanted to get on with the investigation into Billy Hampton's kidnapping, she knew that safety had to come first. No one would be able to help Billy if they weren't safe themselves.

"We'll figure it out," she said to Malik and Samira, trying to project confidence. "Let's get through tonight and see what tomorrow brings."

Fourteen

RAIN FELL GENTLY as Della and Eric stood on the
front porch of the rental house, surveying the storm damage.
Their block had been spared all but some toppled trees.
Sparks from power lines further down the road and the faint
smell of smoke told them they'd been lucky. Neighbors were
stepping out of their houses to assess the situation, too, which
made Della nervous.

"You had better go back inside, Hami," she said. "People
around here know you. They'll recognize you in a heartbeat,
and they'll know you aren't with your wife."

Eric shrugged. "You're right, D., and I should care. Is it
strange that I really don't?"

He kissed her softly on the shoulder as he said it, his arms
wrapping around her trim waist.

Della shivered, both from the cool breeze and the warmth
of his touch. "I'm not sure what to say about that."

Eric nodded but didn't step back. Instead, he leaned
against the rail, positioning himself close to her, their shared

affection visible. "I guess they'll wonder why I'm here without my family. Especially now."

Della bit her lip, struggling to navigate the precarious threads of attraction and professional duty. "Maybe you should go inside. Lay low until we know what's next."

"Maybe," he conceded with a reluctance in his tone. He glanced down the street, where curious neighbors began to congregate. "Do you think they'll talk? About us?"

Della squared her shoulders, knowing this was uncharted territory for them both. "Maybe. I'd prefer we don't give them anything to gossip about."

Eric sighed, raking a hand through his disheveled hair. "It's not fair that our lives become fodder for speculation just because I'm a senator. I wish I'd never taken that job."

"Too late now," Della said, stepping back enough to break the spell that had wrapped around them. "We've got to focus on finding Billy, and if we're seen together too much, people will take it the wrong way."

Eric hesitated, his eyes still searching hers, trying to find a way to bridge the gap of uncertainty. "You make it sound so simple. Being here with you, it feels like I could forget everything else. Not Billy, of course, but you know what I mean. What if things were different?"

Della tilted her head. "What if?"

Their limited vantage point left them unaware just how much damage the tornado had done to the town.

"I mean," Eric continued, his voice softer now, "if things were different, if you weren't worried about the repercussions, would we even be having this conversation?"

"I don't know. Probably not."

As they stepped back into the warmth of the rental home,

Della's thoughts continued to churn. There was something inexplicably magnetic about Eric, a connection that couldn't be easily dismissed.

They settled at the kitchen table, a map of Appleman's Gap laid out before them. Della pulled out her laptop, logged onto the F.B.I.'s network and began reviewing the details and suspects they had gathered. She kept the conversation on track even as she felt Eric's gaze linger on her.

"Let's see what you've got from today," he said, leaning forward with interest as she highlighted the critical points. It was a welcome shift in their dynamic, a sort of unspoken pact to focus on the mission at hand.

Della began laying out the possible leads, not shying away from the information they had collected about Eric's unexpected visitor prior to Billy's disappearance. "We should get a sketch artist to talk to the neighbors who mentioned this stranger," she said. "The other agents might already have that in progress. I'm meeting with them first thing tomorrow morning."

A knock sounded on the front door.

"Who could that be?" Eric asked.

"No idea," Della replied. "Maybe something related to the storm. Stay here. I'll go see."

As Della made her way to the door, a sense of unease washed over her. She took a steadying breath, glancing back at Eric. His brow was furrowed in concern, and she felt the weight of his gaze on her as she turned the doorknob.

The door swung open, revealing Samira and Malik, both dripping from the downpour that had commenced after the tornado's warning had passed. They looked weary yet determined, their faces reflecting the urgency of the situation.

Della had gotten to know them the last time she was in Appleman's Gap. She respected them both. They were good agents, and they'd been an asset to Laurel and Jimmy.

"Agent Brady, you're okay!" Samira exclaimed, stepping inside quickly as Malik followed. "We looked for you at the police station, but the storm made everything chaotic. We figured we'd come over and see if you needed anything."

Della was relieved to see them, especially since they brought with them a sense of normalcy. "I was just getting into a strategy for the investigation. Good timing, agents."

She was wary about letting it be known that Eric was there, but her colleagues would have an ethical obligation to keep the information confidential. What could it hurt?

"Can we help?" Malik asked, shaking the rain from his hair. "We can split the workload if you have leads you want us to chase. Agent Dane went home to get some rest, but we're available, if we can be useful."

When Della opened her mouth to reply, she heard a roaring engine outside. She rushed to the window and pulled aside the curtains. The sight of a police officer's vehicle parked on the street drew her attention.

Della felt her pulse quicken. "Looks like they're here to check up on the damage. They'll likely want to talk to Eric about the situation with Billy."

"Let's not keep them waiting," Eric said, gathering his composure as he joined Della by the window. He straightened, shoulders squared, but there was a flicker of worry behind his eyes.

Della turned to Samira and Malik. "We'll keep things professional as much as we can. Let's highlight the key points from what we discovered earlier about the suspicious person spotted around the community. We need to convey urgency without stirring up unnecessary questions."

Della realized how much she was asking of the young agents. Maybe she was paranoid, but she thought the kitchen still smelled like sex. She and Eric had straightened their clothes, but they hadn't yet freshened up in the bathroom.

"Got it," Samira replied, her voice steady. If she had a reaction to seeing Eric there, she was hiding it well.

The group moved towards the door, and Della opened it to find a short and stocky officer standing on the porch, looking down the street for more signs of damage. He turned at the sound of footsteps and raised a hand in greeting.

"Evening, folks!" he said, tipping his hat slightly to reveal short blonde hair. "We're doing rounds to make sure everyone's safe. Got a few residents worried about the aftermath of the storm. Mind if I step inside?"

"Not at all," Della replied, stepping aside to let him in. "The more eyes we have on the situation, the better."

"We're F.B.I. agents," Malik explained, "working on the Billy Hamilton kidnapping. And this is the boy's father, Senator Eric Hampton."

The officer quickly scanned the room, assessing the unusual gathering. "Sounds like you all are quite the team. I'm Officer Joe Kingston. I was just down the street checking on some folks who had reported damaged property."

"Glad you're on the scene," Eric said. "I've been in contact with your department about my son's abduction, but I was out of town until a few hours ago. I'm scheduled to meet with Chief Tate tomorrow."

Officer Kingston nodded, his demeanor shifting to one of professionalism. "I'm briefed about the case. Anything I can do to help out? We're keeping an eye on the situation, but due to the weather, it's hard to know how far we can extend our resources."

Della stepped forward, pointing to the map they had laid out on the table. "I'm the Special Agent in Charge on this case. We've identified some individuals based on witness descriptions, but we need to coordinate with local officers. There's a possibility that someone matching this profile has been lurking near the Hampton residence."

"Let's make sure we have descriptions, where they were spotted, and any additional details you might find," Officer Kingston said, crossing the room to join them at the table. "Chief Tate will want to be sure the bases are covered."

They nodded their understanding.

"How much storm damage are we dealing with?" Eric asked.

Normally, in the aftermath of a damaging storm, Eric would make a few public appearances to reassure his constituents that resources were available to help them recover. Given his personal situation, though, the optics of that might be tricky.

"I'm not sure yet," Officer Kingston said. "We're working in zones. What I've seen so far isn't bad, but we've only just begun."

As they talked, they heard someone wailing for help outside. It sounded serious. The person was desperate. They all rushed out the front door to learn more.

On the street in front of the house, a young girl stumbled aimlessly. She looked to be no more than 12 or 13 years-old, and her clothing was torn and covered in dirt and blood.

"Help! Please!" she cried, her voice raw with panic.

Della's heart raced as she stepped forward, instinct taking over. "Hey, it's okay! We're here to help you," she called out.

The girl looked up, her wide, frightened eyes scanning the group before locking onto Eric. "My house is gone. My mom and brother ... they're underneath where it used to be."

"From the storm?" Officer Kingston asked, reaching for the radio receiver on his shoulder.

The girl nodded frantically, tears streaming down her dirty cheeks. "I tried to get them out, but I couldn't! Please, you have to help!"

"Okay, we'll help," Della said firmly, stepping closer to the girl. "Can you show us where your house is?"

Without hesitation, the girl turned and began to run down the street, her small frame darting through the debris. Della felt adrenaline coursing through her as she followed, glancing back at the others to ensure they kept pace.

"Stay close!" Della called over her shoulder.

They raced after the girl, who dodged fallen branches and broken structures as they approached the remnants of what had once been a small home. It was now reduced to heaps of debris, the supportive framework splintered and strewn across the yard. A crushing sensation lodged in Della's throat as the full weight of the devastation sank in.

"Dear God," Della muttered.

"Stay behind us," Eric instructed the girl, positioning himself protectively in front of her.

Their faces fell as the reality of the situation sunk in. There was no sign of life near the rubble, and the sound of distant sirens only seemed to amplify their urgency. Gentle rain continued to fall in the darkness.

Della surveyed the wreckage, her heart pounding. "We

need to coordinate a search and rescue operation immediately. There could still be people trapped inside."

Officer Kingston nodded, already on the radio, relaying the information to dispatch. "We have a potential rescue situation on Mockingbird Lane. I need backup and EMS on-site for a neighborhood search. I'm no expert, but it looks like a tornado touched down here."

As they surveyed the scene, they saw more houses reduced to rubble. It looked like a tornado had cut a path diagonally through the town, beginning here and moving northeast.

"Let's start digging," Eric said, rolling up his sleeves, determination etched on his features. "Search and rescue is going to be a while. If there's any chance we can save them, we have to try."

"There's no time to waste," Della agreed.

The young girl clung to Eric's side, eyes wide with fear.

"Stay close to me," he reassured her gently.

The compassion in his voice sparked something within Della. He was not just a senator. Not just a tender lover or an attentive significant other. He was a fundamentally caring man who wanted to help people. He was great with kids, too. She felt a pang of sadness to remember that she could never have children with him. Not biological children, anyway.

As they began to clear away debris, Della took a second to assess the situation. Frantically, she dug her hands into the rubble, pulling away pieces of wood and twisted metal, her mind focused solely on finding survivors.

"Over here!" Malik shouted from the other side of the wreckage. "I think I hear someone!"

Della rushed to his side, and they both leaned in closer to

listen. Sure enough, there was a faint voice muffled beneath the debris.

"Help! Please!" came the weak cry.

"Hang on! We're going to get you out!" Malik called back.

Della redoubled her efforts, tearing away splintered wood and bricks, revealing a narrow space where a woman was partially trapped. "I see her!" Della breathed, panic rising. "Can you move?" she shouted down.

"Barely!" the woman gasped, her eyes wide with fear. "My daughter is inside with my husband!"

"Your daughter came to find us and get you help," Della said.

The woman cried, a sorrowful sound that echoed within the debris. "That was Zoey. She told me she was going for help. My good girl. Her little sister, Maura, is still trapped."

Della's heart sank. They had to act quickly. "We need to clear this area fast!"

Eric joined them, his long, strong arms reaching in as they worked swiftly to pull away chunks of debris. The girl tugged at his pant leg, her voice trembling, "Can you save my mom?"

LAUREL WAS in a state of shock as Officer Matt Wilson pulled up to the driveway entrance at her parents' house and dropped her off. He couldn't get her any closer to the house because debris from the storm blocked the path.

"You sure you don't want me to walk you in?" he asked as they stared at the large, modern farmhouse high on the hill. "It's going to take a while to climb over all those downed trees. In your condition ..."

She waved him off. "Matt, I appreciate your concern. I'm pregnant, not disabled."

The two of them had gotten to know each other over the past few months. They were becoming friends.

He nodded as she got out of the car. "Fine. Call me if you need anything."

"I will."

As she made her way up the long, winding driveway on foot, she saw that Brad's truck was still parked near the house. He obviously hadn't gone back to the station yet. She wondered how he would take the news that she had come to be the bearer of.

A figure emerged from the darkness. Apparently, power was out.

"Laurel, it's so good to see you in one piece," Cornelius called.

His black lab puppy, Sully, woofed his greeting. Sully was growing quickly and finding his place in the family.

"You, too, Dad!" Laurel exclaimed, relieved to hear her father's voice.

Cornelius had been staying in the pool house on his and Maureen's property as he recovered from injuries sustained during Baby Alexia's rescue in New York. He was outside clearing limbs and debris from the walkways, his body strong even though he moved more slowly than he had before. He rushed to hug his daughter as she neared.

"You look like you've been to a war zone, Laurel. What's wrong?" he asked.

"I have been to a war zone," she replied, breaking down into tears. "I tried to go home, and—"

She was interrupted by Brad bursting through the front door. Lilly followed closely behind, woofing enthusiastically. The dog greeted Sully with a sniff of the muzzle and a wag of the tail, but she was most interested in seeing Laurel.

"Babe, you made it!" Brad said, taking his fiancé into his arms. "I haven't been able to get out of the driveway, as you can see. I was just placing some calls to coordinate disaster response as best I can from a distance. I'm glad you're here."

She kissed him and smiled feebly.

"What's wrong?" Brad asked, suddenly realizing that something was.

Anxious for her turn to greet Laurel, Lilly bounced around her ankles. Laurel reached down and scratched the pup on the head. "Hello, girl," Laurel said.

"My daughter was just about to tell me ..." Cornelius added. "She seems rattled."

Laurel stood straight and sighed heavily. She didn't know how to say what she had to, so she decided to do it quickly. To rip the bandage right off.

"I got a ride with Matt," she began. "His car wasn't damaged in the storm, and he offered to take me home."

"Okay," Brad replied, still not sure of the problem. "That was nice of him."

"Yeah, well, when I got to our house—your house, Brad—"

"*Our* house," he corrected.

She nodded, fresh tears welling up in her eyes. "When I got to our house ... I thought I was in the wrong place for a minute ... because it was gone."

"What do you mean?" he asked, his brows high.

"The house is gone. It's nothing but a pile of building materials with a few of our belongings strewn around," Laurel said sadly. "I'm so sorry to have to tell you this."

Brad shoved a hand through his short hair as he worked to process the news.

"What about Jamie?" Cornelius asked. "Was she there?"

Laurel shook her head. "The carriage house only had minimal damage. It looked like anyone in there when the tornado hit would have survived. I knocked on the door, but there wasn't an answer. Was she even in town?"

"I don't know," Cornelius replied, whipping out his phone to contact her. As the mother of his unborn child, he was concerned about Jamie. "She mentioned going to visit her aunt in Alabama again. I'm not sure when—or if—she left."

Cornelius stepped a few paces away as he made the call. No one answered, so he came right back. He looked worried.

Meanwhile, Brad paced around the porch in the darkness.

"What are you thinking?" Laurel asked gently.

Brad took a deep breath, then returned to Laurel and wrapped her in a tight embrace. "I'm thinking that it's just stuff," he said. "We're all safe. Lilly's safe. Most likely, Jamie's safe. The house can be rebuilt. Stuff can be replaced."

Hearing the movement outside, Maureen came out onto the porch. Mack followed closely behind.

It would be the first time Laurel had seen her dad and Mack in the same space. The situation would, no doubt, be awkward, what with Mack taking up with Maureen and staying in the house that she and Cornelius had shared as a married couple for decades. It was a bungled mess, if Laurel did say so herself.

"Laurel, dear, you look like ten miles of bad road," Maureen said as she placed a comforting hand on her daughter's back. "What in the world happened?"

Laurel tearfully relayed the same story about the house being gone. She wasn't comfortable being so emotional in front of Mack, but she figured she had better get used to it. It seemed like he was sticking around for a while.

"It's okay," Brad said. "I'm bummed, but mostly, I'm grateful that everyone is all right."

The porch quickly got crowded as Maggie, Hazel, and Ryan joined the others there.

"What's happening?" Maggie asked.

Maureen shook her head. "Everyone inside. We'll talk there. We have some candles lit in the family room." Cornelius' gaze fell, but Maureen waved him in. "You, too, you old coot."

They followed her, each settling into a comfortable spot. The dogs plopped down around their feet. Not wanting to overstep, Cornelius pulled a single chair from the dining room table to sit on. They caught each other up on the latest as they moved around in the candlelight.

"Now," Maureen said once they were all situated. "First things first. Laurel and Brad, you're staying here for as long as you need. Don't even think about objecting. I won't take no for an answer."

Laurel and Brad looked at each other.

"That's very generous, Maureen," Brad said. "I suppose we should stay tonight, if you don't mind, but we can find a temporary place of our own. We just so happen to have an entire moving truck full of things from Laurel's condo in D.C., and those weren't damaged in the storm. They're safe and sound, parked right outside in your driveway."

Laurel smiled, unsure. She needed time to process, and she wanted to get back to work on the Billy Hampton case as soon as possible.

"Whatever you need," Maureen repeated.

Laurel glanced around the dimly lit room, taking in the faces of her family members. The flickering candlelight cast dancing shadows on the walls, giving the whole scene an almost surreal quality. Despite the warmth of the room and the comforting presence of her loved ones, an overwhelming sense of loss gnawed at her. Their home was gone—a home that held special memories and the promise of a future for her growing family.

The events of the past few hours swirled in her mind. The sheer force of the tornado had reduced their house to a pile of rubble, leaving nothing but debris that would, most likely, have to be trashed. It was a harsh reminder of how fragile life could be. How quickly everything they had worked for could be taken away.

Brad's voice broke through her thoughts. "We'll rebuild," he said firmly, his hand on her knee. "I don't know how long it will take, but we'll make it happen. It'll be even better than before. The house was fully insured."

Laurel nodded, appreciating his optimism. The reality of starting over, especially with a baby on the way, weighed heavily on her. She leaned into Brad, taking comfort in his steady presence.

Maggie, always the practical one, spoke up next. "We'll help. We can all pitch in to make sure you're settled quickly. And if you need anything, just say the word."

"Thanks," Laurel replied, offering her sister a small smile. "I know we'll get through this. It's just ... a lot to take in right now."

As they talked about the logistics of rebuilding and where they would stay in the meantime, Laurel's thoughts drifted to Della. She couldn't shake the feeling that something was off with her friend. Della hadn't been home when Laurel and Mikey had stopped by her D.C. condo the night before, and now, in the quiet after the storm, Laurel's intuition was buzzing. Something was happening, and she couldn't help but worry about her friend.

"Has anyone heard from Della?" Laurel asked, her voice tinged with concern.

Cornelius looked up, shaking his head. "You and Mikey are the only two who keep in close touch with her. Why? Is something wrong?"

"I'm not sure," Laurel admitted. "I just have this feeling ... like she's caught up in something she shouldn't be. I tried calling her, but it went straight to voicemail."

"You know Della," Maggie said, trying to reassure her. "She's probably just wrapped up in work or something."

"Maybe," Laurel said, though the uneasy feeling in her gut persisted. "I think I'll try calling her again later, just to be sure."

As the conversation shifted back to the logistics of dealing with the aftermath of the storm, Laurel's mind wandered. The weather alerts earlier in the day had been a reminder of how unpredictable life could be in Middle Tennessee. Springtime storms were notorious for spawning tornadoes, and everyone in Appleman's Gap knew the importance of taking precautions. But even with all the preparation in the world, there was no controlling the weather. The thought of all the damage added to her growing sense of unease.

"Has anyone checked the orchard?" Ryan asked, echoing Laurel's thoughts. "The apple barn needed a new roof, anyway. I wonder how it held up in the winds we had."

Maureen nodded in agreement. "We've been through rough weather before, but the cleanup this time might be worse than usual."

"Maybe time to go into a new line of work," Mack said with a chuckle.

In response, the room got so quiet, you could hear a pin

drop. The apple orchard had been in the Dane family for generations. None of them had any intention of giving it up.

Cornelius stiffened. It was his family line that the orchard had been inherited through. He already didn't like Mack Roberts for moving in on Maureen, and he didn't take kindly to the flippant comment about the orchard.

"That's not funny," Cornelius said gruffly.

"Agreed," Brad said, his tone serious. "We'll assess everything at first light. But right now, I think we all need some rest. It's been a long day. We can't help ourselves or anyone else without, at least, a little sleep."

Laurel's gaze met Brad's, and she nodded. Rest was exactly what they needed. But as they prepared to settle in for the night, she couldn't shake the feeling that something was looming on the horizon. Something beyond the physical devastation of the storm. Whether it was storm damage or her concerns about Della, she didn't know. But one thing was clear—the challenges they faced were far from over.

As the family members began to disperse, finding their places to sleep for the night, Laurel lingered in the doorway, her thoughts still with Della. She pulled out her phone and sent another message, hoping to hear something—anything— that would ease her worries.

But there was no reply.

With a heavy sigh, she placed her phone back in her pocket and turned to join Brad in her old bedroom. Tomorrow morning, they would begin the process of picking up the pieces and rebuilding what they had lost. Tonight, all she could do was hold on to the hope that, despite the storm and all its destruction, they would find a way to weather the challenges ahead.

Sixteen

AS THEY COMBED through the remains of the frightened girl's house, Della and the team were overwhelmed by the severity of the damage. The roof was completely gone, and what was once a sturdy structure was now a bungled mess. The rain had subsided to a light drizzle, but the ground was muddy, making their movements difficult and the search for survivors even more urgent.

It was remarkable the way a tornado could wipe one house off the face of the Earth and leave another one standing nearby with little to no damage.

Eric, Samira, Malik, and Della fanned out, carefully picking their way through the wreckage as Detective Kingston went back to his cruiser to call for help. The woman they had found was pinned under a heavy beam. It took a while, but Malik and Eric worked together to lift the debris, freeing the woman while Della and Samira reassured Zoey and kept her calm.

"We're going to get you all out of here," Eric promised, his voice steady. "Just stay with us, okay?"

The mother nodded weakly, her face pale with pain but filled with relief as she was finally freed from the debris. "Thank you, Senator Hampton," she whispered.

And just like that, Eric had been recognized. What did he expect?

Zoey ran to her mother, clutching her tightly.

"Is there anyone else inside?" Della asked as she helped the woman sit up, checking for injuries. "You mentioned your husband and another daughter."

It was hard to see much in the darkness of night. If not for the full moon, they wouldn't have been able to see anything at all. They needed powerful flashlights, and fast.

"Yes, my husband and our youngest daughter, Maura," the woman replied, her voice trembling with fear. "They were in the living room, at the front of the house, when the tornado hit. I haven't seen them since."

Eric exchanged a grim look with Della. Time was running out. The house was unstable, and they needed to find the missing family members quickly.

"Let's split up," Della suggested. "Samira, Malik, you stay here and take care of the mother and daughter. Eric and I will search the living room."

They moved quickly, carefully navigating the rubble as they made their way deeper into the house. The destruction was overwhelming, but they pressed on.

As they reached what was left of the living room, Eric spotted a dusty hand poking out from beneath a pile of debris. "Over here!" he called to Della, dropping to his knees and frantically pulling away the wreckage.

Together, they uncovered a man, unconscious but alive,

and a tiny girl, her eyes wide with terror. She clung to her father, her body trembling with shock and fear.

"You're safe now," Della said gently, reaching out to the girl. "We're going to help you and your daddy, okay?"

The girl nodded, tears streaming down her dirt-smudged face as she allowed Della to lift her into her arms. Eric checked the man for a pulse, relieved to find it strong and steady despite his injuries.

"We need to get them out of here," Eric said. "This place isn't safe."

They carefully carried the man and his daughter back outside, where they were reunited with the others.

"We'll get you to safety," Malik assured them as he led the family away from the wreckage. "More help is on its way."

Della knew that there were other people who needed help. Judging from the devastation they'd seen further down the road, there had to be.

"Let's keep moving," she said to the others once the family was safely with Officer Kingston. "There could be people trapped in other houses."

They moved quickly from one damaged home to the next, checking for survivors and doing their best to provide assistance. As they approached the last house in the path of destruction, a chilling sense of foreboding washed over Della. The structure was barely standing, its walls buckling under the weight of the debris. Something about it set off an alarm inside of her.

"Be careful," she warned the others as they approached the entrance.

Eric took the lead, pushing aside the broken door and stepping into the dark, musty interior. The air was thick with dust. As they ventured further inside, Della noticed an over-turned piece of furniture in the center of the room. She wondered if something was hidden beneath it.

She motioned for Eric to help her move the heavy object, and as they lifted it away, a trapdoor was revealed. The wood was splintered and cracked, likely from the impact of the storm.

"Look at this," Della said, her voice barely above a whisper.

Eric knelt down, peering through the broken wood. "There's a basement down there. Or a storm shelter, maybe. "

Della's heart pounded in her chest as she reached for her phone and turned on the light, shining it into the darkness below. The beam of light revealed a set of stairs as the sound of faint cries reached their ears.

"There's someone down there!" Samira exclaimed.

Without hesitation, Eric descended the stairs, the light from his phone cutting through the gloom. Della followed closely behind, and she wished she had her service weapon. Samira and Malik had theirs. A quick glance confirmed for Della that the young agents were thinking the same thing. Their hands were on their guns, and they were ready to use them.

Good.

What they found in the basement made Della's blood run cold.

Huddled together in the corner were several children, their faces pale and eyes wide with fear. Their clothes were torn and their faces were streaked with dirt. But it wasn't just the children that caught Della's attention. There was a man lying unconscious nearby, partially buried under the debris.

Eric froze, recognizing the man's face instantly. "That's him," he said, his voice laced with anger. "That's the guy I saw lurking around my house before Billy was taken."

Della stiffened. "We need to get these kids out of here. Right now."

Eric nodded, his focus shifting to the children. "It's okay," he said softly, kneeling down to their level. "We're here to help you. We're going to get you out of here."

"Is this your dad?" Della asked the kids as she gestured to the man on the ground.

They shook their heads no, though they seemed too frightened to speak. They were young. Perhaps too young to adequately explain the relationship.

"Do you know him?" she tried.

A brave little boy spoke up. "He took us. He wouldn't let us leave here. We want to go home."

Della closed her eyes, her heart sinking. "Thank you for telling us that," she said softly. "You're safe now. We'll get you all home to your parents, okay?"

The kids nodded gratefully, but they seemed too stunned to fully understand what was taking place.

As the group carefully began to lead the children up the stairs, Della instructed Malik to cuff the man on the ground. "We're taking him into custody—unconscious or not," she said. "Senator Hampton ID'd him as the suspect we'd identified, and these kids implicated him. He's done."

Malik nodded, then squatted and cuffed the man.

With a firm grip on the man's wrist, Malik lifted him into a seated position against the wall, ensuring he was restrained. He checked for signs of life but didn't wait for the man to wake. "We'll figure out how to charge him when we get him processed. For now, let's just get these kids to safety."

Della nodded, urging the children ahead of her as they climbed the stairs. "Stay close to me," she instructed, feeling a swell of protectiveness over the weary children. They had endured so much.

As they stepped out into the dim light of the backyard, the ugliness of the storm's aftermath surrounded them. Fallen trees, shattered glass, and the debris of a former life were scattered everywhere. Della glanced at Eric, who had fallen into step beside her.

"Are you okay?" he asked.

"I'm fine," she insisted, leading the children carefully through the yard. A small crowd of onlookers, including Officer Kingston, had gathered, eyes wide and mouths agape as they witnessed the sheltered children emerge from the wreckage.

"Get these kids to the hospital for evaluation," Della instructed Kingston.

"On it," he responded, already pulling out his radio as they approached the others.

It was then that Eric's phone buzzed in his pocket, and he swiftly pulled it out, glancing at the screen before his expression darkened. "I have to take this," he said tersely.

"Eric, wait—" Della started, but he'd already stepped aside, the gravity in his demeanor pulling her attention momentarily away from the kids. Her heart pounded with uncertainty at his growing unease.

"Everyone okay?" he asked, listening intently. Della caught snippets of the conversation, his tone remaining serious.

"... reports of more survivors from earlier found at the police station ... we need to assess the situation ... this won't be over ... I'll be there."

When he hung up, Della looked at him expectantly. Eric took her gently by the arm, leading her out of earshot of the others.

"It was the mayor. The storm caused more damage across town," Eric explained, "plus reports of additional injuries nearby. And heads up—he's calling an emergency briefing for the media at first light. He wants me to appear with him."

Mayor Joe Robinson was a serious, down-to-earth figure with a reputation for being forthright, and he had been a friend to Eric's family despite their recent disputes over political issues.

"At least that means things might be stabilizing," Della said, trying to catch her breath. "Do you really want to be the face of any of this? You have a lot going on."

Eric nodded, acknowledging her point, his brow furrowed in thought. "I need to show that I'm present for my community. Not just as a senator but as a person who cares about their well-being. This isn't a photo op. It's about accountability. If I don't step up, who will? Besides, tonight's find might lead us closer to Billy, right?"

Della admired his fortitude. Here was a man trying to rise to the occasion, despite the personal toll the night had exacted on him. "Yes, absolutely. Just remember to take care of yourself, too."

"Always," he reassured her.

They made their way back to Officer Kingston, who remained on the radio, coordinating efforts and directing traffic while awaiting help and medical personnel.

"Alright, resources are stretched thin, but we have a small medical team en route," Kingston updated them. "Keep the kids calm until help arrives."

Della glanced at Eric. "What's your next step? You had better get some sleep. Morning will come quickly."

Eric's expression was contemplative. "I'm not sure. What about you?"

"I'm heading into the station to see what's left of our case files," Della replied. "Then to the hospital. When our perp wakes up, I intend to be there to question him."

"What about sleep for you? We need to conserve our energy for what's to come." He waved a hand at the debris surrounding them. "There's still a lot of work ahead. How about we get back to the rental house and lay out a plan? We can regroup with the others first thing in the morning."

Overhearing their conversation, Samira and Malik chimed in.

"We've got this," Malik said. "Get a few hours of rest, Agent Brady. We'll handle things from here, then you can relieve us in the morning."

Della nodded reluctantly. She turned back toward the children, who were now surrounded by concerned onlookers. Officer Kingston was on the radio, issuing more instructions as the crowd buzzed with confusion, worry, and fatigue. She felt a swell of both pride and sorrow. The idea of families torn apart—for any reason—weighed heavily on her heart.

"It's all going to be okay," Eric said, locking eyes with her as the sound of approaching sirens began to fill the air.

Seventeen

LAUREL COULDN'T SLEEP. Not with so much to do. She'd dozed a little overnight and was still exhausted, but she had to get back out there to help in whatever way she could. When she returned to the bedroom from the shower, Brad was awake, too. The sun was just beginning to peek above the horizon.

"Up and at 'em," he said with a groggy smile. "What's the order of operations?"

Laurel stood at the foot of the bed, pulling her hair into a messy bun. "I think we should check in with everyone, then assess the damage. I need to reach Della."

Brad rubbed the sleep from his eyes, sitting upright. "Agreed. Let's get organized and head out as soon as we can." He swung his legs over the side of the bed, clearly coming to life at the prospect of action. "Do you want breakfast before we go?"

"I'll take a granola bar or something on the way. I just want to get moving. I'm feeling restless." She paced the small room, her mind racing with thoughts of both the investigation and her family. "We need to know if anyone else was injured in the storm."

"Right. If the damage to our house was severe, there has to be damage to others in the area. I wonder what condition Della is in," he mused thoughtfully. "Let's try to reach her again before we leave."

Laurel nodded, her heart heavy with concern. "I still haven't heard back, which bothers me. It's so unlike her. I want to make sure she's safe. But to be clear, I've been worried about her since she was acting funny in D.C. Whatever is happening with her goes back further than the storm."

Brad showered quickly as Laurel sent Della yet another text. Once they were both dressed and had gathered their belongings, they hurried downstairs to find Laurel's siblings and parents in the kitchen. The atmosphere was busy and hectic, with everyone seeming to plan their next steps despite the early hour and the fact that the driveway was still completely blocked.

Lilly and Sully lounged lazily in front of the sliding glass doors that lead to the back deck. Mack was nowhere in sight.

"Morning, everyone!" Laurel said as she entered.

"Good morning!" her siblings chorused. Maggie and Ryan were already at the table, folding up maps of town and jotting down points of concern.

"I'm so hungry I could eat the north end of a south-bound goat," Maureen mused. "Anyone else want some coffee and toast? It isn't much, but I've got a box of pastries on the counter, too."

Every last one of them said yes. None of the Dane clan would turn down food with such a tough day ahead of them.

"Did you find anything out last night?" Hazel asked, stirring a cup of coffee.

"Not yet," Laurel responded, shaking her head slightly. "Brad and I have plans to check in with everyone first thing, then get a better handle on the damage from the storm and how we can assist."

"Yeah, I wasn't due back to work for another couple of days," Brad added. "I wanted to get the moving truck unloaded. Given the situation, though, I'm going in early. The moving truck can wait."

"I wasn't due back for another couple of days, either, " Laurel added. "In fact, no one told me I could officially work the Billy Hampton kidnapping case yet."

"Like that would stop you," Brad replied.

"What can we do?" Maggie asked, her eyes sparkling with determination.

"You can check on the apple barn and the orchard," Brad suggested with a smile. "Cell phones seem to be working, so let us know what you find."

"Sounds good," Ryan agreed. "I'll work on clearing the driveway today. Do you have a ride? We're all blocked in."

"I already texted Matt," Laurel said. "He should be here any minute."

"Good man," Brad said with a smile. "I'll have to give him a raise."

Laurel laughed softly, glad to feel even a sliver of normalcy amidst the chaos.

"Just be safe, okay? We don't want anyone getting hurt," Hazel reminded

"Of course," Laurel replied, sharing a look of solidarity

with her siblings. "You, too, Hazel. Make sure those crazy cats of yours are all right."

"Crook and Chase are fine out there in the barn. I'm sure of it," she replied. "They're survivors."

Just then, a car horn honked outside. Laurel exchanged glances with Brad.

"That's probably Matt," Brad said, moving toward the door. Laurel followed closely behind.

"Is it okay for Lilly to stay here today?" Laurel asked as she grabbed some toast along with her bag and a jacket. Brad grabbed some, too, popping a piece of toast into his mouth and chewing quickly.

"Of course," Maureen said, wiping her hands on a checkered dish towel. "You two are busier than a moth in a mitten. Leave Lilly to us."

Lilly seemed to smile and nod approvingly from her place on the floor, but she didn't bother to get up.

"Thanks, Mom," Laurel called as they walked out the front door. "See you all later."

Once outside, Laurel was met with the sight of the storm damage in daylight, and it took her breath away.

The landscape was unrecognizable, almost surreal in its devastation. Trees were uprooted, cars lay askew with broken glass littering the ground like confetti, and debris from nearby homes had mingled together in a jumbled mass of colors and materials. The once familiar land around her parents' home now appeared as a battlefield, scarred by the storm's furious rage.

Matt stood next to his car at the bottom of the driveway, waving as they approached. "You ready?" he asked.

Laurel nodded, steeling herself. "Ready as I'll ever be."

Brad joined her side, giving Matt a firm pat on the shoulder. "Thanks for coming out, man. We really appreciate it."

"Of course," Matt replied, his gaze shifting back to the mess around them. "I was already going in for my shift, so it was no trouble. Just doing my job."

Once inside the vehicle, Laurel turned to Brad, who seemed equally pensive.

"I'm glad you're with me today," she said softly, her heart swelling with gratitude. "We'll need each other."

"Absolutely," Brad agreed, meeting her gaze. "We'll take it one step at a time. Keep your phone close and let's stay in touch with family and friends as we go."

As they drove through what remained of Appleman's Gap, they navigated around the debris and fallen trees, picking their way through the destruction with care. Everywhere they looked, the vibrancy of the community had been replaced by a somber atmosphere. The usually bustling streets were eerily quiet, aside from the sound of the occasional emergency vehicle passing by.

"What a disaster," Brad murmured. "I hope no one was seriously injured."

"Me, too," Laurel said, running her fingers across her pregnant belly. "For Billy's sake and for all the families in this town. They've been through enough."

As if on cue, her phone buzzed with a message, drawing her attention away for a moment. It was a text from Ryan.

Just checked the orchard. It's bad. The apple barn is wrecked.

Laurel's heart sank further. A damaged apple barn meant

the potential loss of their family's livelihood, not to mention generations of memories tied to the orchard.

"Everything okay?" Brad asked, noticing her expression.

"Ryan says the orchard is wrecked," she replied. "The apple barn is damaged badly. We'll have to figure out how we're going to right this before harvest season."

Brad nodded solemnly. "We'll get through it. First, let's check in at the station. After that, we'll head over to the orchard. Hopefully, my cruiser is driveable."

"Most of the vehicles in the station lot are okay," Matt said. "They sustained damage, but most looked driveable."

"Good to hear. Thanks, man," Brad said.

Once they reached the police station, Laurel's mind swirled with the events that had unfolded over the past few days—Billy Hampton and the kidnapping, the move, the storm, the house, and now the apple barn. Each concern felt like an additional weight on her shoulders.

"How sad," she mused. "So much fear and loss."

As they stepped inside, they were met by a frenzy of activity. Officers and volunteers scurried around, coordinating efforts to gather resources for those affected by the storm. The atmosphere brimmed with urgency, but as soon as Laurel and Brad walked in, a few heads turned in their direction, and the hustle began to fizz into an eager quiet.

"Agent Dane!" Malik called, waving them over. "We've been awaiting your arrival. We have updates."

"What's going on?" Laurel asked, her eyes sharp with determination.

Malik motioned them closer, gesturing toward a table piled high with files. "First off, we received confirmation that the tornado did indeed cause extensive destruction in several neighborhoods, but we're starting to assess the damage to those affected. The good news? We've managed to locate several survivors who were initially unaccounted for but did get pulled from their homes."

"That's a relief," Laurel admitted. "What about Agent Brady?"

"Agent Aziz and I were with her last night. Last time we spoke to her, she was going to her rental home for a few hours of rest," Malik replied, "but there's been no word from her yet this morning. She's coming in soon to relieve us."

Laurel's brows raised. "Have you been up all night?"

Malik nodded. "Yes, ma'am. Agent Aziz and I both. Duty calls."

Just then, a familiar figure moved through the bustling crowd—Della, looking slightly disheveled but determined. The tension melted away from Laurel's shoulders as she rushed to meet her friend.

"Della!" Laurel called, relief flooding through her as she reached her friend. "I'm so glad to see you! I was worried."

Della embraced her tightly, and for a moment, the world outside faded, leaving only the warmth of their friendship amidst the chaos. "Laurel! I was worried about you, too. I heard about the tornado damage at your place. Are you okay?"

"Yes, we're fine, thankfully," Laurel said quickly, stepping back to gauge Della. "But our house is gone, and so is the apple barn at my family's orchard. We need to figure out how to rebuild. What about you? What happened last night?"

"I can't talk about it now," Della said, glancing around at the officers engrossed in their tasks. "Let's get to work first, okay? We can catch up on everything later."

Laurel nodded, sensing the urgency in Della's tone. "What's the current situation?"

Della motioned to Malik and Samira, who had gathered nearby. "We found children trapped in a house during the storm, but they're okay now. We have another confirmed survivor, and we're working to locate more."

"That's incredible," Laurel said, proud of the team's efforts. "Let's keep that momentum going. We need to get all the information we can about survivors and possible missing persons."

Brad chimed in, "Can someone get me access to any reports from the agents who helped with the recovery during the storm? I need a complete overview."

"Already on it," Malik replied as he flipped through the files on the table. "We've been coordinating with local emergency services for backup and support. They're redirecting aid to families whose homes need immediate assistance. We could use you to help with that, too."

Laurel's heart raced. The need for action surged within her—a mixture of adrenaline and purpose. "Absolutely. I can start reaching out to the families—"

"Not so fast," Della said to her friend. "Let Brad handle the storm recovery. As Chief of Police, that's his job. There's been a break in the Billy Hamilton case that the Bureau needs to focus on."

Laurel stiffened. "Where's Eric?"

Della smiled. "At Mayor Robinson's office. They're holding a briefing any minute now. The news stations out of Nashville are all here for it."

Eighteen

"COME WITH ME TO THE HOSPITAL," Della said to Laurel with a grin. "Right after Agents Washington and Aziz brief us on their progress overnight."

"Okay," Laurel replied. "What's at the hospital?"

"Not what. Who."

"Oh?"

"Remember that suspicious man we identified as a person of interest? The one Eric recognized?" Della asked, her eyes narrowing with purpose. "We found him in the rubble of one of the damaged houses last night. He was unconscious, but alive. He's at the hospital, and I just got word that he's awake. We need to get his statement before he lawyers up or anything else happens."

"We found several kids who say he took them, too," Samira added. "Luck was on our side."

Laurel nodded, the gravity of the situation sinking in. "Wow. Thank God those kids are now safe. We can't let this guy slip away. He might have vital information about Billy's abduction. What's his name?"

Della looked at Samira and Malik, who had been working on ID'ing him.

"Silas Aguilar," Malik said confidently. "He goes by the name Sidewinder. He's from Southern California, and we believe he's working with The Cradler's syndicate. Come, sit down, and we'll get you up to date."

"Sidewinder?" Della asked. "Like the snake?"

"That's right."

"That snake is found where I'm from, in Houston, Texas. Not around here," Della said. "It's a rattlesnake."

"Correct," Samira said. "It's found in desert regions of the Southwestern United States and northwestern Mexico."

"Interesting name for a criminal," Della added.

Della, Laurel, and Brad sat down at the big table in the conference room alongside Samira and Malik, where reports were sprawled out. The atmosphere buzzed with urgency and nervous energy.

"Okay, everyone," Malik started, scanning the room. "As you know, we have a team ready to follow up on any leads from last night. Agents Brady and Dane, your focus will be on gathering information from the suspect and the victims while we coordinate as much as possible with local authorities—namely you, Chief Tate. We know you'll be busy with storm-related recovery, but the Bureau will keep you informed."

"Understood," Brad replied.

He had given up trying to assume control of any investigations related to The Cradler's syndicate. The F.B.I. had taken the lead, and he thought they were doing a fine job. Besides, he had storm damage to deal with right now. Not to mention, his personal issues.

Laurel glanced at Della. "Let's make sure we're both on the same page regarding this Sidewinder character. How do we want to approach him?"

"Based on his previous hostility, we should remain cautious," Della said. "We also need to be firm. He can't be allowed to control the narrative, especially once he realizes we know about the children. He could try to misdirect us. Or worse—he could clam up."

Malik nodded in agreement. "The Bureau has to take the lead on this. It's what we do."

"I guess that means I'm cleared to assist with the case?" Laurel asked, glancing at Della.

"You're here, ready to work, aren't you?" she replied.

Laurel nodded.

"Then yes," Della said with a small smile. "Stop asking ridiculous questions."

They laughed together, releasing some pent-up tension.

"Good work, agents," Della said, turning to Samira and Malik and shaking each of their hands. "Send us everything you have, then go get some rest. I'll see you back here this afternoon."

"Let's move," Laurel said. "Time is critical."

As they walked toward the front door, Della's mind began to whirl with possibilities. She couldn't shake the certainty that the man's connection to Billy's case was deeper than just a casual encounter. The pieces of the puzzle were falling into place, but she needed more information to solidify the truth.

Once outside, they moved toward Della's rental car.

"You have a car?" Laurel asked.

"Of course," Della replied. "Eric and I landed a few hours

before the weather got bad. I'm glad we did. I doubt the rental company has any cars available now. Fortunately, the rental house I'm in didn't sustain any real damage, so the car sat untouched in the driveway."

"Your good luck continues," Laurel mused. "Can you send some of that my way?"

"Yeah, because you aren't lucky at all, Laurel Dane," Della said with a smirk. "Okie-dokie."

As soon as they were alone inside the vehicle, Della knew that Laurel would pepper her with questions.

"So, what's up?" Laurel asked. "And tell me the truth. I know something is going on with you. We've been friends for far too long for you to keep me in the dark."

Della took a deep breath, glancing at Laurel before turning her gaze to the road. "Let's just say that things got a bit complicated between Eric and me. There's a lot of history there, and with everything happening, the emotions started tumbling out."

Laurel shifted in her seat, her expression a mixture of concern and curiosity. "What do you mean by complicated? Did you two—"

"We kissed. At his hotel the other night," Della admitted, cutting off Laurel's question. "It wasn't planned, and it felt impulsive. The connection was always there, hanging between us, waiting for the right moment—or the wrong one, as it seems."

Laurel's brow furrowed with empathy. "I can see how the stress of the situation might bring those feelings to the surface. I think we can agree that Eric is a good looking guy. A good kisser, too, but there's way more at stake for you both than just a kiss. For starters, you've got the investigation, his family, and Billy's case hanging in the balance."

"Right, and that's why I need to stay focused," Della agreed, her voice taut with resolve. "I also know this could put a damper on our friendship if we're not cautious. I might care for him, but I care about you, and about the case, too."

"Della," Laurel began gently, "it sounds like you're feeling torn. It's understandable, given the intensity of everything we've been dealing with lately. Just don't lose sight of what matters. Billy is still out there. You don't want your feelings for Eric to cloud your judgment. Emotional attachments can become liabilities."

Della nodded, grateful for Laurel's support while also acknowledging the truth behind her words. "Says the woman marrying the local police chief. But I know, you're right. I know that when Eric's wife finds out about the kiss, it'll complicate things even more. He can't afford to have his private life turn into public spectacle. Not right now."

"Wait. What?"

Della shrugged, wishing she had said less. "Eric insists he and Sylvia are in a loveless marriage. That they live like roommates. He says she'd be fine with what happened between us."

Laurel looked at her friend with a knowing eye. Something about Della's tone gave it away. "You didn't just kiss, did you?"

Della hesitated, her grip tightening on the steering wheel as she chewed her lower lip. "We ... well, we crossed a line," she finally admitted.

"O-okay. Was this after you had to rescue the kids?" Laurel asked carefully, concern flickering in her eyes. "You were both in a high-stress environment. I want to make sure you understand the ramifications here."

"No, it was before the rescue. Before the storm hit. Well, as the storm was bearing down on Appleman's Gap, actually. I do understand, and it might not have meant anything if the situation hadn't felt so ... charged," Della said, struggling to gather her thoughts. "At some point, I let my walls down. I have feelings for him, Laurel. I always have, even if I tried to bury them. Even when he was dating *you*."

Laurel nodded, a mix of sympathy and worry etched on her features. "This is explosive, Della. You know how volatile his situation is—his career being in the spotlight, the recovery efforts, Billy's kidnapping. You might be walking on a tightrope here."

"I know," Della said, her voice almost a whisper. "I'm telling you, Laurel. What Eric and I have is real, even if it seems reckless."

Laurel shook her head. "That might be true, but you have to think. Billy could be in real danger, and any distraction could put him more at risk. Eric was cleared as a suspect, for now, but he's still under surveillance. You realize that, right? If any of this gets out, it could complicate everything—not just for you and him, but for the investigation itself."

"I have to figure out how to navigate this without compromising my role in the case," Della answered, her voice firm and resolved, but an edge of uncertainty lingered.

"Good," Laurel encouraged. "Focus on the mission. This is a difficult time for everyone involved. You know the pressures of law enforcement. The burden of keeping the public safe is tough for all of us. It's what we signed up for."

Della nodded, her thoughts seeming a world away.

"There's something else I need to tell you," Laurel said. "I wish I could ignore it and pretend I don't know, but I can't."

"Now you're scaring me. What?"

Laurel proceeded to tell Della about Eric's unusual financial records, and she expressed her concerns that he might have been somehow involved with Billy's kidnapping. As Laurel had expected, Della didn't take it well. She adamantly denied any possibility of wrongdoing on Eric's part, and she looked at Laurel like she was crazy for having thought such a thing.

"Forget I said anything," Laurel said to her friend once it became clear that she wasn't getting through.

"I'll try," Della replied.

They parked in the hospital lot, and Della took a steadying breath before exiting the car. The vibrant morning sun shone brightly above—a stark contrast to the darkness of their conversation.

"Are you ready?" Laurel asked, offering Della a moment to gather her resolve.

Della nodded. "Let's do this. We need to find answers."

Together, they entered the bustling hospital, the sterile scent of antiseptic permeating the air. Della led the way toward the admissions desk.

"Excuse me," Della said to the receptionist, who was frantically typing on her computer. "We're looking for information on a patient named Silas Aguilar. He was brought in as a result of the tornado last night."

The receptionist paused, glancing up from her screen. "Can I see your identification, please?"

Della pulled out her badge and showed it to her. "Special Agent Brady with the F.B.I. This is my partner, Agent Dane."

"Okay, let me see," the receptionist responded, typing a few keys before looking back. "He's in Trauma Room 3. I caution you, he's in and out of consciousness. Might be a little while before he can communicate."

"Thank you," Laurel said, leading the way down the sterile hallway. "What do you think will happen once he knows we're here? I hope he doesn't lawyer up immediately."

"Then it's up to us to find the right angle," Della said. "We'll see if we can get something from him before he gets the chance."

They walked in silence, their minds going over potential scenarios. Della felt the familiar thrill of anticipation, knowing they were about to confront the man connected to young Billy's kidnapping. She could only hope he might know where the boy was.

She wanted to do this for Eric. She wanted to be a hero for him.

When they reached the trauma room, Della gently pushed the door open. The room was dimly lit, and Silas Aguilar lay on the hospital bed, unconscious but with medical equipment monitoring his vitals. A nurse moved quietly about, checking the monitors and adjusting an IV drip.

"Is he stable?" Della asked the nurse.

"Yes, he's recovering from a concussion and some bruising. Nothing life-threatening," the nurse replied, glancing up briefly. "I can't wake him for you, though. If you need to talk to him, you might want to consider waiting until he regains consciousness."

"We don't have time to waste," Della pressed. "We could be on a tight timeline here. Can you check with the doctor and see if there's any chance he'll rouse soon?"

"Sure, I'll find out," the nurse said, noting the urgency in Della's tone before leaving the room.

Laurel stepped aside to let Delia focus. She repositioned her jacket and folded her arms across her chest, pacing slightly, as her anxiety heightened. The atmosphere was thick with tension as they awaited the nurse's return.

Della picked up the remote control and turned on the television, just as Eric's press conference was about to begin.

Nineteen

"LOOK AT YOUR GUY," Laurel said, nodding up at the TV. "He's a handsome one, you know."

Della nodded. "That, he is."

Laurel placed a hand on her pregnant belly. It was a pose she found herself in a lot lately. She felt more connected than ever to the little one growing inside of her.

"Look," Della added. "Your guy is there, too. They look good."

Laurel followed Della's gaze, and there was Brad, standing tall in his police uniform and looking official alongside Eric and Mayor Robinson.

"It's odd that we both dated Eric, but haven't really talked about it," Laurel said softly.

"I agree," Della said, glancing at her watch.

She wished they could get on with questioning Sidewinder, but figured that since they had time to kill, she and Laurel might as well talk.

"Why did you two break up?" Laurel asked, not realizing it was a touchy subject.

"That's a long story," Della replied. "Why did you break up? You're the one who broke up with him, right?"

Laurel nodded. "Yeah, it was my doing. It wasn't any one thing, really. It just wasn't the right fit. At some point, I realized that I would miss out on the guy who was right for me if I stayed entangled with the wrong one. Eric and I were great as friends. We never should have been more. I met Brad not long after we broke up, so it all worked out for the best."

Della smiled, then looked down at the floor. Her story was so much more complicated.

Noticing her friend's sadness, Laurel said, "When we were together, he often talked about you."

That got Della's attention. She looked up, her eyes alight. "He did?"

"He didn't say your name. He just called you 'D.' It wasn't until you and I became friends that I realized the connection."

Della's heart raced, a rush of bittersweet memories flooding her mind. "I never knew he still thought about me after we broke up. I thought I faded from his life once he moved on."

"He never spoke poorly of you," Laurel said, her voice laced with kindness. "Not once. He clearly respected you."

Della hesitated, a pang of longing washing over her. "I often think about what might have been. When we were together, I wanted to be the one for him. But I knew he wanted a child. It wasn't meant to be, I guess." She looked down again, biting back tears.

Laurel reached over, squeezing Della's hand. "You both were different people then. Maybe you are meant to revisit that connection now, under these circumstances."

Before Della could respond, the nurse returned. "The doctor says he should be waking up soon, but with how groggy he is, I'm afraid the sedation will take a bit longer to wear off," she said. "You can wait with him if you like."

"Thanks," Della replied, her voice steady. "We will."

As the nurse left, silence enveloped the room, punctuated only by the beeping of machines. The image of Eric delivering his speech filled the screen, the camera panning across the assembly of reporters eager for answers.

"We want to reassure the citizens of Appleman's Gap that we're working around the clock to search, rescue, and locate missing persons," Eric said, his voice confident and sincere. "We've mobilized teams to ensure swift action, and I will remain here to monitor the progress.

"In the face of this devastating tornado, our community's strength and resilience have never been more evident. We are coordinating closely with local and state authorities to provide immediate relief and ensure that every affected individual receives the support they need. Our first priority is the safety and well-being of our residents. Search and rescue operations are currently underway, with dedicated teams combing through the affected areas to find and assist those who may still be trapped or in need of urgent care.

"Additionally, we are setting up emergency shelters and providing essential supplies such as food, water, and medical aid to those who have been displaced. The response from our emergency services, law enforcement, and volunteers has been extraordinary, and their bravery and commitment should be a source of pride for all of us.

"I want to emphasize that the recovery process will take time, and we are committed to standing by you every step of the way. The Federal Emergency Management Agency is already on the ground, assessing the damage and beginning the process of providing disaster relief funds to help rebuild our homes, businesses, and infrastructure. The U.S. Army Corps of Engineers is also assisting in clearing debris and restoring critical infrastructure.

"To those who have lost loved ones, homes, or businesses, please know that you are not alone. We will do everything in our power to help you recover and rebuild. We are a resilient community, and we will come through this stronger than ever.

"I urge everyone to follow the instructions of local authorities, stay safe, and look out for one another. Together, we will overcome this disaster, and Appleman's Gap will emerge from this stronger, united, and ready to rebuild. Thank you, and may God bless our community and guide us through these challenging times."

Della felt pride swell within her. The way Eric spoke, so passionately about his community, only cemented her feelings further. He always had that fire—one that attracted people and inspired bravery in others. No way could she imagine him being involved with his own child's kidnapping.

"It sounds like there's more pressure on him than ever," Laurel noted, a hint of trepidation in her tone. "Do you think he'll be okay after everything?"

"He's more than capable," Della replied, her gaze locked on the screen. "But the more public scrutiny he faces, the more complicated our situation becomes. I worry about how we'll handle this once everything is revealed."

As if on cue, the door to the room creaked open, and an older doctor walked in, followed by the same nurse. He approached Silas Aguilar's bed, flipping through a chart while glancing between the patient and the agents. "Hello, agents. Thank you for your patience. I understand you wish to speak to Mr. Aguilar."

"Yes, that's correct," Laurel replied. "Is he ready to talk?"

The doctor lowered the chart and looked serious. "He's regained consciousness, but it might take some time before he's fully coherent. We need to assess his condition first."

He was repeating what they'd already been told. That wasn't very helpful.

"Can we at least ask him a few preliminary questions?" Della pressed. "It's urgent."

He sighed, weighing the situation carefully. "I suppose you could ask him a couple of questions. But be gentle. He's been through quite an ordeal. Don't push him too hard."

"Thank you, Doctor," Della said earnestly.

Laurel stepped forward, inching closer to Silas' bedside. "If someone could get him to agree to talk, it might be a life-saving conversation."

"All right then," the doctor said, stepping back. "Good luck."

As Silas stirred slightly in the bed, Laurel took a breath to steady herself. She was about to connect with a man who might hold the key to everything. Della stepped closer, her eyes focused intently on the scene unfolding.

"Mr. Aguilar?" Laurel said softly, leaning over the bed. "Can you hear me?"

His eyelids fluttered, revealing a hazy gaze. "Wh-where am I?"

"You're in the hospital," Laurel replied carefully. "You

were in an accident during the storm last night. We need to ask you some questions about what happened."

Silas's eyes widened, confusion taking over his expression. "What about the kids?"

"What do you know about them?" Laurel pressed, her voice firm but gentle.

Silas struggled to sit up. "Where are they? Are they okay?"

"They were found alive," Laurel reassured him, meeting his gaze steadily. "But we need your help to understand what happened. Can you tell us what you remember?"

Silas's brow furrowed as he tried to piece together his memories. "I ... I was just going to grab something from my car when the tornado hit. Everything went dark. Then I was in someone's house ... there were kids ..." His voice trailed off, fear creeping into his tone.

Laurel leaned closer. "You were in the basement of a house with several children. Can you remember why you were there?"

Silas shook his head slowly, his breaths becoming more labored. "I ... I didn't mean for any of this to happen. They wanted to lay low. I was only supposed to check on them."

Laurel exchanged a glance with Della. "Check on who? Who were you working for?"

Silas shifted uncomfortably, glancing at the door as if expecting someone to burst in. "You don't understand ... it wasn't supposed to happen like this. I didn't want things to escalate."

"Escalate how?" Laurel pressed, her voice firm. "What did you mean by 'lay low'?"

Silas swallowed hard, panic washing over his features. "I was just a temp. I wasn't meant to get involved. I didn't want any trouble. But they said ... they said there was a job, and I needed the money. I've only been on it a few weeks."

"Who set up the job?" Laurel demanded, her instincts kicking into high gear. "Who were you working for, Mr. Aguilar?"

"That's not what this is about." He paused, the urgency in his eyes growing more frantic. "They'll kill me! They'll kill all of us if I say anything!"

Laurel frowned, exchanging another worried glance with Della. "We can protect you. But you need to come clean about everything you know. This is important for your safety and the safety of those kids."

"I-I can't," he stammered, the fear consuming him. "You don't understand. I saw things. Things I wasn't meant to. They'll come looking for me. They'll find me!"

"Who will?" Laurel pressed, her patience beginning to wane. "Mr. Aguilar, you need to trust us. We're here to help. But we can only do that if you give us the information we need."

He hesitated , glancing nervously at the door once more, as if expecting someone to burst in and silence him. "There are people who don't take kindly to loose ends," he finally admitted, his voice barely above a whisper.

"Tell us who they are," Laurel urged gently but firmly. "We can protect you. But we need names and details."

Silas' breathing quickened, and he looked torn between fear and desperation. "I don't know if I can trust you," he murmured. "What if you are connected to them?"

Laurel steadied her gaze on him. "You already know we're not here to harm you. You were found unconscious in the wreckage. We're from the F.B.I. We're here for the children.

They're counting on you. Don't let fear force you into silence. Who is after you?"

He seemed to consider her words. After an eternity, he spoke again, his voice barely audible. "They work for The Cradler—all of them. Kidnapping kids, selling them to the highest bidder. I thought I could keep my head down and avoid the drama, but it always finds you ... even when you run."

Laurel felt a chill run down her spine at the name. "Where is Billy Hampton? You have to tell us everything you know," she urged.

Silas flinched at the mention of the boy's name. "I didn't know they were taking kids from families until it was too late. Billy was one of the first since I've been involved ..." He paused, his eyes darting around the room again. "I heard them say he would be kept at a safe house until the deal was finalized."

"Where?" Laurel pressed. "Where is the safe house?"

Silas shook his head, seemingly terrified. "I don't know! I swear! They were talking about it in code. I overheard bits and pieces. All I know is they were all paranoid about him being found. They'll kill anyone who crosses them. Especially me."

"Listen to me," Laurel said, her voice lowering to a more calming tone. "If you give us the information we need, we can do our job. We can help you get to safety. But you must cooperate. We'll offer you protection if you tell us everything you heard."

Silas hesitated, staring at them with wide eyes. Slowly, he nodded, as if coming to a decision.

Twenty

DELLA STEPPED IN, happy to play the bad cop.

"Mr. Aguilar," she said, her voice sharp now, "this is your last chance. If you don't start talking, you could die in here. You have no idea what you're up against."

He looked shocked, eying Laurel's pregnant belly. "Are you ladies threatening me?"

Della and Laurel didn't answer, their expressions serious.

The fear in his eyes intensified. "Okay, okay! Just don't hurt me," he pleaded, hands trembling slightly. "I'll tell you what I can. But I need your protection first."

Della exchanged a quick glance with Laurel before responding. "You'll have our protection, but you need to give us something tangible. You must answer our questions honestly, if you want to stay safe."

Silas took a deep breath, clearly on the edge of panic. "I only know what I've overheard. The Cradler has several safe houses across the region. It's all part of a network—houses where they move the kids around to stay hidden. They move them often. Billy was meant to be kept in a house near the old highway, out by the quarry. That's what I remember."

Della leaned closer, her eyes narrowing in focus. "Do you have an exact location? We need more than just a vague idea of where to find him."

"One of the places has been used three times. It's always abandoned when they move the kids. I overheard them mention it close to the town's border, just off County Road 17. I'm pretty sure they have to stick to isolated places to avoid detection," Silas rambled, almost in a desperate urgency.

Della felt a rush of adrenaline. "Can you be more specific?"

Silas looked wistful, a flicker of recognition crossing his face. "It's a specific landmark. An old church. The old Chapel of St. Bethlehem. That's where I think they take them when the deals are set. I overheard a plan for Billy, making arrangements. They weren't careful. 'He's going to be a prime piece,' they said as he'd draw a good price—especially with the media attention," he added, his voice trembling as he glanced nervously around the room, as though he feared someone would eavesdrop.

"A church?" Della breathed, her heart racing as she turned to Laurel. "That's not far from here. If they're using that as a drop-off point, we could get a team together and ambush them before they make a transfer."

Laurel's mind whirled with the implications. "We need to confirm this information first, but if he's right, it could be our best lead yet. We should mobilize our resources and prepare for a raid."

"Let's do it," Della agreed.

She walked over to the window and looked out at the

parking lot below. She wasn't looking for anything, in particular, but she could almost feel The Cradler making plans to thwart their efforts. It sounded like Sidewinder was a key part of his syndicate. They'd need to move fast.

The Bureau still didn't know where the kids they'd found in the tornado wreckage had come from. There were no reports of currently missing children in Appleman's Gap, except for Billy. A team was in the process of checking the national database maintained by the National Crime Information Center (NCIC). Most of the kids found after the tornado were too young to provide their addresses, parents' names, and in some cases, even their own last names. There was much more to uncover, and Silas Aguilar was the best lead they had.

"Keep calm, Mr. Aguilar," Della said, returning her focus to him. "We're going to act on this, but if you mislead us, there will be consequences. Remember that your safety depends on what you tell us."

Silas nodded vigorously, eyes wide with fear. "I swear I'm telling the truth! Please—I just want out of this mess."

Della's gaze sharpened. "Good. You keep your head down and cooperate, and we'll protect you."

Just then, the nurse reentered the room, her expression puzzled as she surveyed the expressions on their faces. "Is everything okay in here?"

"Yes, thank you," Della replied, giving her a quick smile. "We're just wrapping up our conversation with Mr. Aguilar."

"All right. He needs to rest now that he's regaining consciousness. We need to monitor him for any aftereffects of the sedation," she said gently.

Della nodded, keenly aware of the clock ticking down on their lead. "Of course. Thank you for your help."

Laurel stepped back, turning to Della. "Let's go. We have enough to act on."

"Wait!" Silas said anxiously. "What about me? You can't just leave me here alone. They'll come for me."

"We'll send two agents to stand guard outside your door," Della said. "No one will harm you with them here."

"Then will you wait with me until they get here?"

Della and Laurel glanced at each other. It wasn't an unreasonable request. Eric's press conference was still on TV. They were taking questions now, and eager reporters were shoving microphones in his face.

"I don't mind. For a few minutes," Laurel said. "We can watch the news."

Della nodded. "Okay. Let me step outside and make a phone call to arrange for the security detail. Be right back."

She did, and it was less than twenty minutes before two beefy agents arrived to stand guard. They were from Nashville and had been called in early this morning to help. They had gotten to Appleman's Gap just in time.

As Laurel and Della exited the trauma room, Della could hear the bustling noise of the hospital's emergency services outside. She felt another surge of adrenaline, anticipation rushing through her veins now more than ever. Their investigation had taken a step forward, and the thought of possibly rescuing Billy was within reach.

"Does this feel right, Laurel?" Della asked. "Can you believe the connection to the chapel he mentioned? If we follow up, we might be able to turn this around."

"Absolutely," Laurel replied. She had heard classical music

as they were questioning Silas. "We need to approach it cautiously, though. We have to keep our wits about us. We might not know how many people are involved in this plot, or what we're dealing with once we show up."

"Right. Safety first," Della agreed as they arrived in the lobby.

"Let's check with Headquarters and see if we can get a team rolling on this lead,"

The urgency in Della's tone mirrored the commotion buzzing around them.

Laurel's heart raced in sync with her thoughts. To think they were on the brink of a breakthrough in such a daunting case brought a sense of warmth to her chest. Progress was happening fast.

"Hey," Laurel said, catching Della's gaze. "I know how heavy everything feels right now. If we manage to rescue Billy, it'll mean the world to us and to everyone affected by all of this madness."

Della nodded. "You're right. We won't give up now. Not when we're so close. Just don't suggest to me that Eric was involved. Okay?"

Laurel nodded, wishing she'd never mentioned her suspicions to her friend.

"I know I told you a little about this," Laurel said, "but I was kidnapped as a child. Those memories are slowly coming back to me. I don't know for sure who was responsible, but Dad thinks it was The Cradler's father, Lucian Somerset. Lucian died in prison. If we can take The Cradler down, it will feel like a personal victory for me, you know? Even if we get just one of his goons. It's all good."

"I know," Della replied. "Finding Billy will feel like a personal victory for me, too. I want to do that for Eric."

"I know."

Just then, a commotion erupted from the entrance of the hospital. A group of reporters, having caught wind of Della and Eric's relationship, surged toward the doors, their cameras flashing like lightning.

"Looks like they know something," Laurel said, an eyebrow raised.

"Let's hope I can stay composed," Della replied. "I'll need to."

Her phone buzzed in her pocket with a call from Eric. Turning away from the crowd, she answered, placing one finger in her ear to block out the noise.

"Hami, what's going on?" she asked.

"Just listen, he said, his tone apologetic. Are the reporters there?"

"Yes."

"They're asking questions about us, D," Eric said quietly over the phone. "They know we were together last night, and they're putting pieces together. It's only a matter of time before they start speculating publicly."

Della's stomach churned. "Do you think they'll start a smear campaign?"

"They might," Eric replied. "But I don't think they're ready to go that far. Right now, it's about optics—people are starting to wonder why I'm not with Sylvia. This could get messy."

Della exhaled slowly. "I'll handle it. Just stay calm and focus on Billy. We need to keep that front and center, no matter what."

"I'm with you," Eric said, his voice steady. "Be careful out there. If they keep pushing, it might distract from the investigation ... and the storm recovery efforts."

Della nodded to herself. "I'll keep it professional. You do the same. Make sure the press knows that finding Billy is the priority. We'll meet up this evening."

Ending the call, Della turned back to Laurel, who had been watching the reporters with a furrowed brow. "We need to keep the focus on the case," Della said. "The more they dig, the harder it'll be to keep mine and Eric's relationship out of the spotlight."

And there it was. Della had just called her situation with Eric a relationship. She smiled a small smile as she heard the words tumble out of her mouth.

Laurel nodded, her hand absentmindedly rubbing her belly. "Let's get ahead of this. The last thing we need is the media muddying the waters while Billy's still out there."

The reporters outside were buzzing, cameras flashing as they pushed microphones toward the entrance, hoping for a soundbite from anyone inside the hospital. Della caught a glimpse of their eager faces through the glass doors, their attention fixed on the exit like vultures circling a potential meal.

"Let's leave quietly," Della suggested, eyeing a side door that led to the parking lot. "We don't need to make a spectacle."

Laurel agreed, and together they slipped out of the hospital unnoticed, the warm spring air hitting them as they stepped into the parking lot. They walked quickly to the car.

As they drove toward the police station, the streets of Appleman's Gap were eerily quiet, the aftermath of the storm still visible in the form of downed power lines and scattered debris. The landscape was a stark reminder of the town's vulnerability—both from the forces of nature and the sinister forces at play in Billy's disappearance.

"You ready for this?" Della asked, breaking the silence. "With your house and your family's apple barn destroyed, no one would bat an eye if you took some time away."

Laurel glanced at her. "I don't know if anyone can ever be ready for something like all of this. But time away isn't an option until the child is found. We're getting Billy back. No matter what."

Della nodded, her expression resolute. "Let's get to the station. We need a solid plan before we make our move."

When they arrived, the building was a hub of activity. Agents, officers, and emergency responders were scattered throughout. Della and Laurel made their way to the conference room, where they were briefed on the situation.

"We've got a team ready," one of the agents said as he handed Della a tablet. "We've confirmed some movement near the old chapel on County Road 17. It matches the description Aguilar gave."

Della's heart raced as she scanned the information. "Looks like we've got a window. Let's set a time and get our units ready. I want eyes on that chapel."

Laurel was already coordinating with the tactical teams, her voice steady as she relayed instructions. "We need to approach quietly. If Billy's in there, we can't risk them moving him again."

The plan was set in motion quickly, the tension mounting as they prepared for the raid. They were close—so close—but one wrong move could mean the difference between saving Billy and losing him forever.

Twenty-One

THE REST of the day was a flurry of activity. Between the investigation into Billy's disappearance, the handling of the kids that had been found amongst the rubble, and recovery efforts after the storm damage, Appleman's Gap was busier than it had ever been. The few hotels in town were completely booked, and those in nearby towns stretching from Lebanon, Mount Juliet, and Hermitage to the west and Cookeville to the east saw a noticeable surge.

It was after midnight by the time Laurel's head hit the pillow at her mom and dad's house.

"What a day," Brad said as he fell into the bed beside his fiancé and pulled her close.

Lilly climbed onto the bed and nestled in between them, happy for her parents to be home. Her soft, spotted head rested gently against Laurel's knees.

"You can say that again," Laurel replied. "Days like these are exhilarating, but I can't help but think it would be an easier pace if I worked with Dad and Mikey. I'm not sure I can keep this up once the baby gets here."

Brad sighed. "I'm glad to hear that. I've been worried about you, but I didn't want to say anything. You're burning the candle at both ends."

"I know. It's hard to slow down. To accept this new phase of my life," Laurel said. "I'm happy about our baby on the way and all of the steps forward, but it's also a loss for me, you know? I'm losing the person I was before."

Brad squeezed her and kissed her gently. He didn't say anything else. What could he say? His life was changing, too, but not in the same way.

"Speaking of a loss, how are you feeling about the house?" she asked.

Brad sighed again. "Like I said, it's just stuff."

"Yeah, but it was mostly your stuff," Laurel said. "Are you sad?"

He hesitated, collecting his thoughts. "I am sad. It's a bummer, for sure. But I like to keep the big picture in mind. I'd trade all of that stuff and more for you and our baby in a heartbeat. You're safe. That's all that matters."

Lilly squirmed and let out a groan, as if to ask, "What about me?"

"You, too, sweet girl," Brad said to the pup.

"So, where are we going to live?" Laurel asked. "I believe Mom when she says we can stay here as long as we want, but I'd like to be in our own space before the baby comes. Wouldn't you?"

"I would."

"Then what's the plan?" Laurel's eyelids fluttered, drifting closed.

Brad watched her for a few minutes as she drifted off.

Suddenly, she jerked awake again. "I remembered something today," she said groggily.

"Yeah? What."

"From when I was a kid. When I was … taken."

Brad scooted even closer, sensing the seriousness. He'd wondered if pregnancy was somehow serving to make Laurel remember more about her childhood trauma. He didn't understand how that worked, but he wanted to be there for her as best he could.

"If you feel like it," he said, "tell me about it."

"It's nothing major," she replied. "Just a memory of Dad showing up and carrying me out of some dingy house. I'd never been more relieved to see him. He was wearing his police uniform, and I remember the feel of the radio on his belt. It scraped my shin as he hoisted me onto his shoulder. I didn't even care. The pain barely registered."

"I'm so glad Cornelius found you," Brad said. "I can't imagine what he must have gone through. Maureen, too. It's every parent's worst nightmare. Now, becoming a dad myself, it terrifies me."

Laurel nodded. "I agree. I already feel so protective of this baby. Like, I'd fight a wild lion … if I had to."

"You wouldn't have to, because I'd fight it for you," Brad replied.

Laurel smiled, her eyelids fluttering shut again. "That's why we have to bring down The Cradler. I don't think I'll rest until we do."

"I hear you," Brad said softly, waiting to see if she was asleep. When she opened her eyes again, he continued. "Hey, babe, losing the house made me think … anything can happen at any time. I don't want to wait to marry you. Especially with this baby on the way. I don't need a fancy wedding. I just want you to be my wife. I want us to be a family."

"We are a family."

"You know what I mean," he continued. "Officially and legally."

Laurel roused, propping herself up on one elbow. "I kind of feel the same way."

"Then let's get married!" Brad shouted, so loud that Lilly lifted her head and woofed her agreement. "I've been waiting what feels like forever to make you my wife. I don't want to wait another day."

"When?"

"Tomorrow."

Laurel smiled. "Are you serious? With everything going on, our house destroyed, and the town in shambles, you want to get married ... tomorrow?"

"Yep. Right here, at your parents' house. We can do it out back by the pool. The view of the orchard in the distance won't be quite the same with the apple barn collapsed, but these are the hills and the trees that nourished you all of your life, Laurel Dane. This ground is where everyone you love calls home. Even if they live somewhere else, this is where their hearts are. I'm honored to join your big, boisterous, beautiful family. Let's get married. Right here. Tomorrow. Make me the happiest man in the world."

Laurel raised a hand to her mouth, her cheeks flushing. "I'm not sure what Mikey has going on. The kids are in school. What if he can't make it?"

"He'll be here," Brad said. "Call him now. Or I'll call him."

"I can call him."

"Della's in town," Brad continued. "Ryan is home on spring break. Cornelius is alive. It's perfect timing, really."

"Are we really doing this?" Laurel asked.

"Yes, we are," Brad replied, his eyes sparkling with joy. "Let's not waste any more time. We've both been through so much already. Let's get married and celebrate the life we're building together."

Laurel's heart raced, caught in a whirlwind of excitement and determination. "You're right. Let's do it. I want to marry you more than anything."

She grabbed her phone, quickly texting Mikey.

> Are you and the fam free tomorrow? Brad and I are getting married at Mom and Dad's. Be there!

"Done," she said, looking up at Brad with a grin. "Now, what about my dress? I can't get married in sweatpants!"

"Oh, I've got that covered, too," he said, standing up. "I'll make a few calls while you shower and get ready in the morning. There are bridal shops still open downtown. If they're open, we'll fetch a dress that suits you. And then we'll have a tiny, beautiful ceremony right here."

"What time?"

"How about late afternoon? 4pm? That gives everyone enough time to get here, and it ought to be warm enough."

Laurel's heart soared at the thought. The changes in her life had been dizzying, but despite the whirlwind circumstances, she was excited about marrying the love of her life. "I can't believe this is happening."

Brad smiled. "Believe it. We'll make this happen. Our

family deserves to see that we're committing to each other, regardless of the circumstances."

She nodded, her mind racing with all the things she had to do before the ceremony. "All right, the preparations will be quick. Don't forget about the dogs. Lilly is going to want to be included. Sully might as well be, too. He's family."

"How about this? I'll take care of everything else," Brad assured her. "You handle yourself. We'll meet in the backyard at 4pm, and it will be special, just like you."

With that, Laurel shot off a few more texts to her family members, Della, Kanesha, Sarah, and even Samira and Malik, her heart racing with anticipation. She rolled over to try to sleep, a chorus of thoughts racing through her mind. Would her parents approve? What would the neighbors think?

Deep down, she knew that what truly mattered was their love and commitment to each other.

"Okay, okay, let's seriously do this!" she said aloud, shaking off the worries as she finished up.

They stayed up for several more hours, caught in a whirlwind of excitement and planning. The soft glow of the moonlight filtered through the curtains, and Lilly had curled up again between them, seemingly oblivious to the monumental plans her parents were making.

Brad shifted slightly, propping himself up on his elbow to face Laurel. "Babe, are you sure you're good with this? We can wait if you're not ready. I don't want to pressure you."

Laurel turned her head to look at him, her eyes soft but resolute. "I'm sure. It feels right. I've been holding onto this idea of the perfect wedding for so long, but the tornado put everything into perspective. I don't want to wait anymore."

Brad reached over and gently stroked her cheek. "I feel the

same way. Nothing else is guaranteed, but I want you by my side through whatever comes next."

Laurel nodded. "This baby, Brad ... it's already changed everything. Today, when I thought about all the kids they found in the storm, I kept imagining what it would feel like if it were our child in danger." She paused, glancing down at her belly. "I already love this baby so much."

Brad's hand moved to rest on her belly, gently caressing the bump that held their future. "We're going to be great parents, you know that? And we're going to figure it all out."

Laurel let out a soft laugh, shaking her head. "I hope so. It's just ... I've always been so driven. My career, the F.B.I., everything I've worked for—it's been my whole life. Now, I feel like I'm entering a whole new chapter, and it's scary. What if I'm not good at balancing it all? What if I'm not ready to let go of the person I was?"

Brad leaned in, pressing a kiss to her forehead. "You don't have to let go of who you are. You're still going to be an amazing investigator—whether that's for the Bureau or your own agency. Just like you're going to be an amazing mom. And hey, if you do decide to go into business with your dad and Mikey, I'll support you every step of the way."

Laurel smiled, feeling a sense of comfort wash over her. "Thanks, babe. I needed to hear that." She shifted in bed, turning to fully face him. "So, logistically speaking ... how are we going to pull this off tomorrow? We're talking about getting married with no preparation. I feel like I should be panicking, but I'm actually kind of excited."

Brad grinned. "That's the spirit. Don't worry about a thing. Like I said, I'll make some calls in the morning. Maybe your mom will help me. I think she knows everyone in this town. You just focus on getting ready and staying relaxed. We're keeping it simple, but it'll still be beautiful. I promise."

Laurel raised an eyebrow. "You're really going to take care of everything? Flowers, food, all of it?"

"Absolutely," Brad replied confidently. "I've got it under control. You've had enough on your plate. Let me handle the details. I did okay with the quintet gig the other night, didn't I?"

Laurel's heart swelled with affection for him. "You really are amazing, you know that? I don't know what I'd do without you."

He smiled softly, leaning in to kiss her again. "You'll never have to find out. Now, let's try to get some sleep. We've got a big day ahead of us."

As they settled back into bed, Laurel smiled. Everything was falling into place, even in the midst of the havoc surrounding them. She rested her hand on her belly, feeling the gentle flutter of movement from the baby inside her.

Life was moving forward, no matter what.

Brad pulled her close, wrapping his arms around her as Lilly nestled between them once more. They lay in comfortable silence for a while, until sleep beckoned them both. Before she drifted off, Laurel whispered, "Thank you, Brad. For everything."

Twenty-Two

"HAMI, WAKE UP," Della said to the sleeping figure beside her in the bed. "It's time."

Eric stirred, blinking against the sunlight streaming through the window. "What time is it?" he muttered, his voice thick with sleep.

Della checked her watch, the anxiety of the day ahead settling in her stomach. "Almost seven a.m., which is eight a.m. in D.C., sleepy head. We need to get moving. We have a lot to do before the press conference."

Eric sat up, running a hand through his messy hair, the memory of last night flooding back. The conversations they had shared, the weight of his responsibilities. "Did I really fall asleep? I was planning to catch up with you about the chapel lead," he said.

"You did. I thought maybe you needed it," she replied, smiling softly. "Now, we need to gather everyone and touch base."

Eric nodded, the weariness leaving his expression as

purpose began to replace it. "You're right. Let's get ready and head to the station."

Eric stretched, his hand brushing against Della's arm as he moved. The warmth of his touch lingered, sending a spark of electricity through her. She glanced down at him, noticing the way his sleepy eyes softened when they met hers.

"I can't believe I actually slept," he said with a chuckle. "I guess I'm more exhausted than I realized. Or maybe I'm relaxed when I'm with you."

"Exhausted or not, we've got a full day ahead," Della replied, her tone teasing but gentle. She reached out, playfully brushing a stray lock of hair from his forehead.

Eric caught her hand before she could pull it back, his fingers curling around hers. "You've been so good to me, D," he said, his voice low and sincere. "I don't know how I'd be handling all of this without you."

Della felt her cheeks pink at the sincerity in his tone. "You'd find a way," she replied softly, her gaze meeting his.

Even as she said it, she knew that wasn't entirely true. There was something about their connection, something that had been reignited after all these years, that made it clear they leaned on each other in a way they hadn't in the past.

Eric's thumb traced small circles over the back of her hand. "Yesterday, when you were working, I couldn't stop thinking about you," he confessed. "About us."

Della's pulse quickened. She had been trying to focus on the case, but Eric had a way of drawing her in, making her feel like the rest of the world melted away when they were together.

"Hami, we're walking a dangerous line," she said, her voice barely above a whisper. "You're still a married man."

"I know," Eric said, his tone serious but tender. "I don't want to pretend anymore. I talked to Sylvia last night. I asked her for a divorce."

Della's eyes widened in surprise. "You what?"

Eric sat up straighter, turning his body to face her fully. "I can't keep living like this, trapped in a marriage that's been dead for years. It's not fair to Sylvia, and it's not fair to me. I need to move on. To be with someone who makes me feel alive again. To be with *you*. I never should have let you go."

Della searched his eyes. "Are you sure about this? I mean, what about your next reelection campaign? And the press? They're going to have a field day with it."

Eric's expression softened, his thumb still tracing gentle patterns on her hand. "I don't care. I can't keep living for appearances. I don't want to waste any more time pretending to be someone I'm not. And the truth is, I want to be with you. I've always wanted to be with you."

Her heart raced at his words, her mind spinning with the implications. Part of her wanted to throw caution to the wind and let herself fall into him completely, but another part—the rational, professional part—kept her grounded.

"We can't just dive into this. We have a lot to figure out—"

"I know," Eric interrupted, his voice soft but insistent. "I know it's complicated, but we've both been waiting long enough, haven't we? I don't want to wait anymore. Not when I finally know what I want."

Della hesitated, her emotions warring inside her. She had spent years trying to bury her feelings for him, convincing herself that they had made the right decision to go their separate ways. Now, with Eric sitting in front of her, telling her he wanted a future with her, it was harder than ever to deny the pull between them.

"I care about you, Hami," she said softly, her voice catching in her throat. "But I can't just ignore everything else. We have Billy to find. We have responsibilities."

Eric leaned in closer, his eyes locked on hers. "We'll find Billy. When we do, I don't want to go back to pretending that we're just colleagues, or that I don't feel this way about you. I want you to meet my son, and I want him to know that you're the special lady in my life. He might be young, but he's old enough to realize that his mother and I aren't happy together. We aren't in love with each other."

Della leaned into his touch, her forehead resting gently against his. "It's not going to be easy."

"I know," Eric whispered, his breath warm against her skin. "Nothing worth having ever is."

For a moment, they sat there in the quiet morning light, their foreheads pressed together, their feelings filling the space between them. Della closed her eyes, allowing herself to imagine what it might be like to finally let herself love him again. To embrace the future he was offering.

"I want to be with you, too," she whispered, her voice barely audible.

Eric smiled, pressing a soft kiss to her lips. "Good."

The tension between them lingered, a promise of what could be, but for now, they had to focus on the day ahead. Della took a deep breath, pulling back slightly and giving him a playful nudge. "We need to get to the station. The press conference isn't going to wait for us."

Eric chuckled, his hand lingering on hers for a moment longer before he reluctantly let go. "You're right. Duty calls."

Before they could get out of bed, Della's phone buzzed on the nightstand with a notification. Swiping to unlock the screen, she saw that it was the Ancestry service she'd sent her DNA sample to.

"What's that?" Eric asked when he saw her face light up. "Good news, I hope."

"Oh, it's nothing, really," she replied, quickly logging in and navigating through the screens as she searched for the status window.

"It doesn't look like nothing."

She smiled, giving in. "I sent a DNA sample away to one of those labs. I've been wanting to learn more about where I come from. I don't even know who my biological father is. Mom won't tell me. She gets all weird whenever I ask about it. I have his last name, but that's all I know."

"Good for you, D.," Eric said. "You have my full support, of course, in anything you want to do. Are your results ready?"

Della's face fell as the page loaded and she learned that the results were still pending.

"Not yet, apparently," she explained. "Looks like the alert is because the lab received my sample and is processing it. Oh, well."

Eric gave her arm a gentle squeeze, showing his support. "Soon," he said.

Noticing the text from Laurel, Della smiled. "There's something else."

"Good news, I take it, by the look on your face?" Eric asked.

Della nodded, then held the phone out for Eric to read.

"Laurel and Brad are getting married this afternoon. They want us to come."

"Wow!" Eric said, his expression one of genuine happiness. "Those two are made for each other. I'm glad they're getting married sooner rather than later. I mean, it's been—what?—six or seven years that they've been together, right?"

"Something like that, yes."

"Good for them," he said.

"Does that mean you'll come with me?" she asked. "You know, I wouldn't miss it. Four o'clock at her parents' place."

He pulled her close and kissed her. "I suppose, it would be an opportunity to go semi-public as a couple."

"Or we could lay low and act like colleagues who are attending a friend's wedding," Della said.

"What's the fun in that?" he asked playfully.

She shrugged. "We have a few hours to think about it. Just promise me you'll be there, okay?"

He nodded and smiled. "Assuming we can't do anything specific to help Billy during that hour, then of course. I'll be there."

As they got up and began getting ready, there was a newfound sense of clarity between them. They had both been dancing around their feelings for far too long, and now, they had a chance to face them head-on.

They headed out the door, ready to tackle the challenges ahead, and only somewhat worried about being seen together. Something had shifted between them. It felt right.

Arriving at the station, they were greeted with a scene of coordinated chaos. Officers were on the phone, barking orders, while others scurried in and out with files and equipment. Della felt the familiar rush of adrenaline as she absorbed the electric atmosphere. They were fighters in a battle against the shadows that lurked in this community—Eric's community. It was a community that deserved so much more than this turmoil.

"Della! Eric!" Laurel called out as she approached, her voice slicing through the din. "I'm so glad to see you both."

"Right back at you," Della said, her heart warming at the sight of her friend, who seemed both excited and nervous. "You look beautiful. What are you doing here, though? How are the wedding plans coming along?"

"Pretty well, actually," Laurel replied, a smile brightening her features. "Everyone took the news surprisingly well. Mom and Dad are practically giddy with the preparations. We just need the final touches—which Brad is taking care of—and then it's all about gathering our most special people. The orchard is going to be one hell of a backdrop for the ceremony."

"Why just the orchard?" Eric asked. "I think the whole town should come and celebrate."

"Right? They all sort of have a stake in this love story," Laurel laughed. "It's a community affair. But I'm focused on doing what I can on the investigation before I have to get myself ready for the wedding."

"Is it possible to juggle both?" Della asked. "If anyone can do it, it's you, but we've got things covered here."

Laurel's smile faltered slightly. "Yeah. It's just that we're so close to finding Billy. I can feel it."

"From your mouth to God's ears," Eric said. "I want my little boy back."

Laurel nodded. "We'll do everything we can to make that happen. We're close to making our move."

"Speaking of which," Della said, pulling out a tablet, "we've got a lead on the chapel. It seems potential targets are lining up, but we need to parse the details carefully. If Sidewinder has mapped this out, we'll pull a team together for a joint operation. Maybe tonight, under the cover of darkness?"

"Great!" Laurel exclaimed, excitement bubbling up. "Let's run through the details again. I'd love nothing more than to end my wedding day with the news that Billy was found, safe and sound."

Realizing their conversation held depth beyond just a wedding and an investigation, Eric took a deep breath. "We're talking about a community that needs closure—not just on the tragedy of the storm but on the ongoing threat of this kidnapping syndicate. Bringing Billy home can start the healing process that Appleman's Gap desperately needs."

Laurel smiled. "Exactly. Families deserve answers, and they need hope. Finding Billy doesn't necessarily mean finding The Cradler. His reign of terror has gone on far too long, and it's probably not over yet. If we can show that we stand united, it will sharpen our strategy moving forward and give us greater resolve."

Della glanced at Eric. "If Billy's at the chapel, we need to act tonight to rescue him. Every minute counts, and we can't risk the syndicate catching wind of our plans. We will go in with a strong team. If anything goes south, we'll adapt."

Just then, the phone in Laurel's pocket buzzed, interrupting their planning. She pulled it out, seeing it was a text from her friend Kanesha.

> Saw something strange at Jack and Jill's.
> Can you talk?

Laurel's stomach dropped. "Wow ..." she whispered as she continued to read the message. "Did they really do that? Someone is getting careless."

"What's wrong?" Della asked, stepping closer.

Laurel's fingers moved across the screen as she continued to read the text.

> I think there's evidence of a getaway driver's car at the dock near the restaurant. I don't know what y'all have going on right now, but I wanted to tell you in case it has something to do with that boy's kidnapping. My sister would want me to help put a stop to this.

"Kanesha Sneed found an abandoned car at the lake near Jack and Jill's restaurant, where she works," Laurel explained, voice tense. "Someone left it behind, and she thinks it's suspicious. Kanesha has become a friend of mine. She proved her knack for finding clues when Jasper Hobbs was missing, then sadly, her sister, Tiana Sneed Douglas, was killed and her baby cut from her womb. I've learned to trust Kanesha's instincts. She has a personal stake in seeing The Cradler's syndicate brought to justice."

"Can we get a unit out there?" Eric asked, his expression turning serious.

"I'm on it," Della said confidently. "Laurel, get out of here and get yourself dolled up for that wedding. We've got this. I promise."

Twenty-Three

DELLA MOVED QUICKLY, collaborating with Samira and Malik to divide and conquer.

They pulled together a team to head to Jack and Jill's, strategizing a plan to investigate the abandoned vehicle Kanesha had reported. Meanwhile, another team began to plan the raid of the chapel that would take place after dark tonight. The urgency in the air was palpable, each agent aware that time was of the essence.

Eric headed to the mayor's office to prepare for today's press conference. He winked and blew Della a kiss when he left. Her colleagues pretended not to notice.

"Remember, we need intel," Della said, her voice steady as she addressed everyone in the briefing room. "This could lead us directly to The Cradler, his associates, or Billy Hampton. We'll conduct a raid of the chapel tonight. If Billy is there, we need to seize the opportunity while we can. The more evidence we have on hand when we do it, the better."

"The car could be a crucial piece of the puzzle," Malik

added, scanning the files. "Or it could be nothing, but I prefer to be hopeful. It feels like we're close."

Della nodded, her mind focused on the possibilities. "Absolutely. Let's keep our options open. With the storm damage, we can't count on anything to be as it seems. This might be a diversion or smokescreen."

"Or it could be a result of the storm," Malik said, playing devil's advocate. "Maybe the car got tossed there in the high winds."

"Right. Let's hope it's something more," Della replied. "We could all use a win."

Agents began to gather equipment, ensuring they had everything they needed.

With a plan in place, they split into teams—one going to check the car at the lake, while the other coordinated with local police for the chapel raid later that evening.

As Della stepped outside, her mind was a whirlwind of thoughts. She couldn't shake the lingering worry about the situation with Eric and how easy it had been to slip back into old feelings. She was afraid of how Sylvia would react and how the media might spin things. With the case at stake, though, she had to focus on what was crucial. That's why she was in Appleman's Gap in the first place.

On the drive to Jack and Jill's, the streets echoed with signs of recovery. It was evident that the community was resilient. Neighbors helped one another, clearing debris and checking in on each other. She had to admit that Appleman's Gap was a charming little town. In the aftermath of the storm, the locals were living up to the volunteer spirit Tennesseans were known for. Even though she realized the idea sounded crazy, Della thought that she could live here one day.

Arriving at the restaurant, Della parked and stepped into the area where the car was reported. The faint sounds of laughter from patrons enjoying the aftermath of the storm grazed her ears, a poignant reminder of the life that continued even in the face of tragedy.

A group of uniforms stood clustered by a nondescript sedan parked haphazardly between two trees, its paint chipped and covered in mud.

"That's it," Malik said, signaling her over. "Kanesha wasn't wrong."

Della stepped closer as the officers examined the vehicle. "What do we know so far?" she asked, crossing her arms and taking stock.

"The plates match a stolen vehicle report from earlier this month," one of the officers stated, entering the information into the system on his police laptop. "Looks like it's connected to an organized crime syndicate operating in the area, tied to The Cradler. The owner was last seen in Nashville."

A rush of adrenaline coursed through Della. "Do you have CCT footage?" she asked, her heart racing at the implications. "This could tie back to Billy."

"We're checking the cameras from nearby businesses," an officer said as he surveyed the vehicle. "We've put out a statewide alert for this plate already. The stolen vehicle might have been used for a pickup of the kidnapped kids."

"Let's get a couple of officers to canvas the area," Della instructed.

Malik nodded, pulling out his phone to make the call as Della took a closer look at the sedan.

"Check the trunk," she ordered. "I want to see if there's anything inside."

The officers exchanged glances but complied, one of them retrieving the keys from the ignition and opening the trunk. A mix of dirt and dented metal greeted them, but it was the images of a few hastily discarded bags and boxes that garnered Della's attention.

"Careful. This could contain evidence," she warned as an officer leaned in closer.

As he shuffled through the contents, Della's pulse quickened. There were clothes—a child's shirt, something bright and whimsical—and several plastic bags containing snacks, likely thrown together hastily. A few were marked with logos of popular brands she had seen in grocery stores.

"Agent Brady!" Samira called out, returning with fresh intel from the cameras. "There are feeds showing this car being parked here just hours after the storm struck. We should have a clearer timeline."

"Did you see who parked it?" Della asked as she moved closer to Samira, eyes sharp with determination.

She shook his head. "Not a clear shot, but we've identified a white pickup that was seen circling the area before the car arrived. It fits the description of another suspect linked to some previous criminal activity."

"Great. That gives us something solid to pursue," Della said. "Let's gather all this evidence and move quickly."

The officers began cataloging the items in the trunk, making notes, while Samira worked diligently to pull the security feeds that might connect the dots. Della's thoughts raced as she considered how close they were to uncovering the truth.

"This will be good. I can feel it," Della said, fiery determination igniting within her. Each new piece of information tightened the thread that would soon solve the case.

As they continued to sift through the contents of the trunk, Della's mind spun with possibilities. The clothes and the snacks painted a picture of children. If there were more kids involved and if the trunk was used for transporting them, there might be forensic evidence that could lead to a break.

Just then, her phone buzzed again. Della snatched it from her pocket, seeing that it was a text from Eric.

Press conference at 11. Mayor wants to update the public on progress since yesterday. Can you be there?

Della sighed. The press conference would be crucial for maintaining public trust and reassuring the town of Appleman's Gap that the authorities were doing everything in their power to find Billy Hampton and take down The Cradler—not to mention, handle storm recovery—but the timing couldn't be worse.

She quickly typed back.

I'll try, but we just got a new lead. I might be late.

Her phone buzzed again almost immediately. This time, it wasn't Eric. It was a number she didn't recognize and hadn't expected.

It's Sylvia. We need to talk.

Della's stomach dropped. She had known this moment would come, but now, with everything hanging in the balance, it felt like one complication too many.

Malik approached her, noticing the tension on her face. "Everything okay?" he asked.

"Just fine," she replied, slipping her phone back into her pocket. "We need to keep pushing forward with the investigation. I'll catch up with Eric later."

The last thing she needed was to let personal drama affect the case, but the looming confrontation with Sylvia weighed heavily on her mind.

An hour later, after wrapping up the investigation at Jack and Jill's, Della made her way toward the mayor's office, arriving just as the press conference was starting. She slipped through the crowd, standing near the back as Eric took the podium. His voice was strong, commanding the attention of everyone gathered.

"We want to reassure the citizens of Appleman's Gap that we're working around the clock to search, rescue, and locate missing persons," Eric said, his voice confident and sincere. "Since yesterday, we've made significant progress in our investigation. Several key leads have been uncovered, and our agents are following up on them as we speak."

Della watched him, admiring how natural he was in this role—an authoritative figure who inspired confidence. He wasn't saying much different than he had in the press conference the day before, yet the townspeople who had gathered seemed to want to hear from him. They looked to him for comfort during this frightening time.

Underneath that professional facade was the man she loved. The man who had now told her he was leaving his wife.

The thought made her uneasy, especially knowing Sylvia was nearby and wanted to talk to her. What could she possibly have to say to Della, if not to accuse her of breaking up the marriage?

Eric continued, "We've mobilized teams across the region, and with the support of local law enforcement and the F.B.I., we are confident that we will bring Billy home. As for storm damage, authorities believe they have completed their search and rescue efforts and are now in the clean-up phase. FEMA is still in town and is providing assistance as quickly as they can. I will remain in Appleman's Gap to monitor the progress personally. I know this has been a difficult time, but help is here."

The crowd murmured as reporters shouted questions. Della could sense their anticipation, the desperation to hear that something—anything—was being done to resolve the crisis.

As Eric stepped down from the podium, Della's phone buzzed again. This time, Sylvia's message was short and direct.

I'm outside the mayor's office. I'll wait.

Della exhaled deeply. She didn't want to face Sylvia, but she knew she couldn't avoid it forever. She watched as Eric disappeared into the mayor's office, surrounded by aides and local officials, still unaware that his soon-to-be ex-wife had arrived.

Gathering her courage, Della made her way outside. Sure enough, Sylvia stood by her car, her arms crossed, wearing an expression that was both stoic and tense. Her dark hair was pulled back into a neat bun, and her eyes were sharp and calculating. Although they'd never met in person before, Della recognized her from pictures she'd seen on the internet. Della was embarrassed to admit that she'd followed Eric's family more closely than she probably should have over the years. She'd wished that it was her with Eric and a happy little boy instead of Sylvia. Seeing the woman in the flesh made Della feel guilty for that.

"Della," Sylvia said as she approached, her voice even. "We need to have a conversation."

Della nodded, bracing herself for what was to come. "I figured as much."

The two women stood there for a moment, sizing each other up in the warm spring air. Sylvia finally broke the silence. "Eric asked for a divorce."

Della wasn't sure how to respond, so she said the only thing she could. "Yes. He told me."

Sylvia's gaze didn't waver. "I don't care if you two are together, Della. I've known about your history for a long time. I'm not here to accuse you of anything. That said, the optics of this are dangerous. Eric's a senator. His career—and our public image—matters."

Della appreciated Sylvia's candor, but it didn't make the situation any less complicated. "I understand the optics, Sylvia. Trust me, this isn't the way I wanted things to happen."

Sylvia's lips tightened into a thin line. "Well, it's happening. And the press is going to pick up on it. You both need to be careful. This is about more than just your personal lives. It's about Eric's career and the stability of the town."

"I know," Della said quietly. "I don't want to make this harder on him, or you."

Sylvia's expression softened, just a fraction. "I'm not here to fight you, Della. But I won't have this blow up and hurt our reputations. Eric and I will handle the divorce quietly, but you need to make sure he doesn't let his personal feelings get in the way of his responsibilities. This town needs him to be focused."

Della nodded. "He's committed to the investigation and the storm recovery. Those are his priorities right now."

"Good." Sylvia's voice was firm. "Because this town can't afford any more distractions. It might not matter to you, since you don't live here, but it matters to me."

With that, Sylvia returned to her car, leaving Della standing there, rattled and feeling like she'd been scolded.

Della took a deep breath, trying to steady herself. She hadn't expected the conversation to go that smoothly, but it was clear that Sylvia's concerns went beyond the personal.

The stakes were high, and the last thing anyone needed was a scandal overshadowing the work they were doing investigating The Cradler's syndicate. He would continue to terrorize innocent families until he was found and brought to justice. Della could never forgive herself if her choices slowed progress.

Twenty-Four

"IT LOOKS AMAZING ON YOU," the owner at Lakeside Lace said as Laurel twirled in front of the full-length mirror.

The woman beamed from her position in the corner of the room, almost as if she knew Laurel personally. She did—sort of. Lacey Johnson had gone to school with Maureen, way back when, and she'd always remembered her fondly. When Maureen had called and asked Lacey to fit Laurel for a last minute wedding gown, Lacey had been delighted to help an old friend.

"Thank you," Laurel said, blushing.

She was a blushing bride.

Finally, she thought.

"It looks like it might need a few minor alterations to hug your baby properly, but my seamstress can do those right away. What time do you need the dress?"

Laurel looked down at her watch, raising a brow. "At the latest, three o'clock," she said. "Is that possible?"

"Consider it done," Lacey said. "It will be our honor to be part of your special day."

"You're the best," Laurel said.

Laurel took another twirl, the soft fabric of the wedding gown brushing against her legs as she moved. The dress was breathtaking, a vision of delicate lace and silk that seemed to shimmer with each turn. Its empire waistline flowed perfectly over her growing belly, giving her an ethereal, goddess-like appearance. The gown's creamy ivory hue contrasted beautifully with her sun-kissed skin, and the intricate lace detailing around the bodice drew attention to her neckline and shoulders.

The fabric clung softly to her curves, accentuating her shape without constraining her. A ribbon of satin tied just beneath her bust, drawing attention to her pregnancy and symbolizing the love she and Brad shared for the little one growing inside her. Laurel ran her hands over the smooth material, marveling at how the dress managed to make her feel both graceful and powerful, like the bride she had always envisioned.

Behind her, the full-length mirror reflected not just her image but the happiness and anticipation glowing in her eyes. Her hair cascaded in soft waves down her back, a few tendrils framing her face, ready to be tucked behind her ears or pinned up into the loose updo she had planned. The gown's delicate train swept the floor behind her, trailing just long enough to add a hint of drama without being cumbersome.

The softest layers of tulle peeked out from beneath the lace overlay, giving the dress a dreamy, almost weightless quality. As she spun, the dress flared out slightly, giving her a glimpse of the barely visible lace appliqués embroidered into the skirt. It was as if every inch of the gown had been crafted with her in mind, designed to fit her new role not just as Brad Tate's wife, but as a mother-to-be.

"It's perfect," Laurel murmured, turning her head to the side, trying to take it all in.

The dress made her feel beautiful in a way she hadn't expected. Being pregnant had sometimes made her feel awkward and uncomfortable in her own skin. But this gown? This gown made her feel radiant.

Lacey smiled warmly, her eyes soft with admiration. "You look like a vision, Laurel. And the best part? That dress is designed for moments just like this. It's crafted to move with you, to accommodate your changing body, so you'll be comfortable."

Laurel's heart swelled. She looked down at her belly, imagining the tiny life inside her. "It's amazing," she said again, voice softer now. "I was worried it would be hard to feel bridal, you know, with the baby and everything."

"Oh, honey," Lacey said, stepping forward, her voice full of affection. "That baby makes you even more beautiful. You're glowing in a way only a mother can."

Laurel's eyes misted as she imagined walking down the aisle toward Brad, their family surrounding them, and this tiny miracle cradled inside her.

"I can't wait for Brad to see you in this," Lacey added with a wink. "He's going to be completely smitten."

Laurel smiled, her mind already racing ahead to the ceremony. "This is definitely the one," she said, her heart thumping in her chest. "I'll take it."

As she stepped down from the platform, the seamstress whisked in to make a few quick adjustments. Laurel felt a sense of peace wash over her, knowing that everything was falling into place.

"Is there anything else I can help you with today, dear?" Lacey asked.

"Actually," Laurel replied, "do you know anyone who could do my hair last minute?"

Lacey hesitated for a moment.

"If not, it's no problem. Just thought I'd ask."

"I know someone," Lacey said. "Let me make a call."

She disappeared behind the sales counter as Laurel took off the gown and got dressed in her street clothes. By the time Laurel stepped out of the dressing room, the gown on a hanger, Lacey wore a huge smile.

"Well?" Laurel asked. "Do tell, Ms. Johnson."

"I spoke with my cousin at Tress Lounge, downtown. They're slower than usual due to the tornado. She says she can get you in, if you go right away!"

Laurel practically jumped up and down, surprising herself at how much she felt like a giddy schoolgirl. She'd waited on this day for so long. She could hardly believe it was finally here. That things were falling right into place as if they had been planning for a year.

Sometimes, you're in the flow, and the flow feels good.

"That's amazing!" Laurel said. "I'll head right over. What's your cousin's name?"

"Stevie. Same last name as me, so Stevie Johnson. Be sure to tell her I sent you," Lacey said. "When you're done, come back here, and your gown should be ready."

Laurel paid for her dress and thanked Lacey with a hug, then she got into her car and drove the short distance downtown. She'd passed the Tress Lounge many times, but hadn't been inside. It had tons of curb appeal, with its wooden sign hanging above the glass door and fresh flowers visible on a table in the bay window.

"In we go," Laurel said to the baby as she parked and walked inside. "Ms. Stevie is going to make Mama look pretty for the wedding to your daddy."

Stepping into Tress Lounge, Laurel was immediately enveloped by the warm scent of hair products and the gentle hum of chatter and laughter. Bright mirrors adorned the walls, reflecting the cheerful and welcoming ambiance. Stylists moved about, expertly working with clients to craft gorgeous hairstyles.

The place was impressive, especially for a small town like Appleman's Gap. Laurel's tiny hometown was becoming polished into quite the gem. Seeing this made her feel good to have moved back, even if her house was destroyed and most of the belongings she and Brad still had sat on a moving truck in her parents' driveway.

"Welcome!" a chipper voice called from the front. A woman with curly hair and vibrant pink highlights approached, her hands dusted with a fine sheen of product. "How can we help you today?"

Laurel smiled, enjoying the friendly atmosphere. "Hi! I'm here to see Stevie Johnson? Lacey sent me."

"Oh, absolutely! Come right this way!" she said with an inviting smile, leading Laurel toward the back of the salon past stylist stations and chairs filled with clients.

Soon enough, they reached a low-smoked glass station where an older woman with sleek shoulder-length hair was arranging her tools. "Stevie! This is Laurel," the hairdresser said with a practiced wink. "She's the one Lacey called about."

Stevie turned with a grin, her smile brightening the room. "Lacey is a sweetheart. I'm glad you came in! How can we get you looking fabulous today?"

Laurel chuckled, her excitement bubbling over. "I need a hairstyle for my wedding today. It's last minute, but I'm hoping you can work some magic."

"Of course! Let's do something that brings out your natural beauty," Stevie replied, her hands already moving with purpose. "Take a seat, and we'll figure out what style suits you best."

As Laurel settled into the chair, she reflected on how surreal everything was. The stress washed away under Stevie's skilled hands as she leaned forward to examine Laurel's hair.

"What's your vision for today? Are you looking for something elegant and sophisticated, or maybe a playful touch?" Stevie asked, her eyes twinkling with creativity.

"Oh, I'm thinking something natural but beautiful, maybe an updo with some soft strands framing my face," Laurel replied. "I just washed and blow dried my hair this morning."

Stevie nodded, her fingers twisting and pinning Laurel's hair into a chic updo. The skill and speed with which she worked made Laurel feel at ease. With each twist and adjustment, she could see the transformation taking place.

"I must say," Stevie said as she worked, "you have such a beautiful face. The updo will definitely show off your features."

Laurel smiled, her heart fluttering at the thought of Brad seeing her in the dress. "Thank you. It means a lot after everything that's happened. It feels good to focus on something joyful."

Stevie began to spritz hairspray, locking the style into place as the salon's atmosphere buzzed with cheerful chatter. "Know what? You're doing great. This whole 'let's rush for a wedding' attitude is exciting and probably helps you take your mind off the bad stuff."

"Yeah, exactly. I've been so focused on the uncertainties in my life lately." Laurel sighed, gently leaning back in the chair as she caught Stevie's eye in the mirror.

"It's about balance. Weddings can be stressful but fun at the same time, especially with family around to celebrate. Embrace it. This day is yours!" Stevie waved her arms playfully. "Plus, your little one is going to add a whole other layer of joy to your wedding."

To Laurel's surprise, the woman with the pink highlights reappeared. "Sorry to interrupt, but you have a visitor."

Laurel's eyes widened when she saw none other than Mikey Dane sauntering her way. Her brother was the absolute best.

"Mikey! What are you doing here?" she asked with a grin.

"Hey, Sis," he said as he leaned over to hug her. He plopped down in an empty chair and shoved a hand through his blonde hair. "Since none of the women in our family saw fit to accompany you, I figured I'd step in. Do you mind?"

"Not at all," she replied. "They're all getting themselves ready for the ceremony. I understand completely. But I'm glad you're here. How did you find me?"

"Easy. Mom sent me to Lacey's, then Lacey sent me over here."

"I wasn't even sure you could make the ceremony on such short notice," Laurel said. "Knoxville isn't too far away, but it isn't right around the corner, either."

"You knew I'd be here."

"Jess and the kids, too?" Laurel asked.

Mikey nodded proudly. "The whole gang. And by the way, you look beautiful."

As Stevie finished the final touches, Laurel felt herself beaming from ear to ear. The weight of the tumultuous days melted away, giving way to a bright hope.

"I agree with your brother. You look absolutely stunning!" Stevie declared with pride as she spun the chair around to face the mirror. Laurel gasped at her reflection.

"I love it. Thank you so much!"

"Of course. Now, what time is your wedding?"

"Four o'clock!" Laurel exclaimed. "I must hurry back. My family will be at my parents' house, helping to set up. You have no idea how much this means to me."

"Then go! You're going to shine like a diamond!" Stevie cheered, waving her hand.

Twenty-Five

"WHAT WAS THAT ABOUT, D.?" Eric asked as Della returned to the building. He'd been waiting for her after the press conference, and had apparently seen her and Sylvia talking.

She took a deep breath, knowing the conversation would need to be handled delicately. "We had to talk about ... well, about us. Sylvia wanted to make sure we both understood the complications. The media is going to dig into our connection at some point, given the timing."

Eric nodded, his jaw tightening slightly. "I figured as much. When those cameras were on me, it felt like the whole world was watching. I don't think it matters, though. Sylvia has agreed to a divorce."

"I'm glad for that. I don't want our relationship—however it's defined—to hinder our work."

"Right, of course." He turned his gaze toward the bustling activity outside. "We've already lost time. Let's make sure we don't waste any more."

"Agreed," Della replied, gathering her thoughts. "I need to

coordinate with the teams at the station about the raid tonight. Don't forget, we have a wedding to attend."

"Sounds like a plan," Eric said, his voice steady. He seemed to settle into a state of resolve that Della found comforting. "I'll focus on storm recovery and see how I can be of use. Are we riding to the Dane house together?"

"Sure. Pick me up around three thirty at the rental house?" Della asked. "I need to change into something more appropriate for a wedding."

"It's a date, D.," he said with a smile. "I can't wait to see what you wear."

They worked their respective tasks throughout the day. Knowing each was out doing what they could to help brought them closer together in their efforts.

As Della moved through her day chatting with officers and locals from the community, all of them expressed support for Eric and his family. It made her proud to see how much they cared about their senator. By all measures, he was a good man.

She kept glancing at her phone, hoping to see a message from him. Time passed quickly, the hours blurring into one another as they moved deeper into the heart of the investigation.

Not long before Della planned to leave for the rental house and a change of attire, her phone buzzed. She pulled it out and frowned at the unfamiliar number. Tempted to ignore it, she glanced up and saw Malik approaching.

"Got a lead?" he asked, nodding toward her phone.

"I don't recognize the number," she said, her brow furrowing. More curiosity brewed than fear. "Might be a tele-marketer or a wrong number. I guess I should check."

"Go ahead," Malik said. "It's mostly a waiting game until the raid tonight, anyway. Forensics is processing the car."

"You're right," Della said. Then, "Hello, you've reached Della Brady."

"Um, hello," a timid voice said on the other end of the line. "Is this Della Brady?"

"That's right," Della said, wondering who in the world this was and why she was making her repeat herself.

"Um, my name is Cate Brady," she said. "Well, actually, it's Cate Fredericks now. I'm remarried. It used to be Cate Brady."

"Okay," Della replied, confused.

She'd been desperate to learn more about her biological father's family, and hearing from someone with the same last name was intriguing.

"I got an alert this morning from my husband's ancestry account. I still check his email," the woman said, before correcting herself. "Actually, he's my former husband. My first husband? It's weird. I don't know how to describe him anymore."

Della stiffened. She'd received an alert this morning, too, but she hadn't seen her DNA results. Had she read them wrong? "Yeah?" she asked.

"Anyway," Cate continued, "the alert said that you were his biological sister."

Della gasped, the news hitting her like a punch to the gut. She was excited, but this had come completely out of left field. She was in shock. "I'm sorry. I'm his what?"

"Sister," Cate said. "He never knew about you. Did you know about him?"

"No," Della replied. "What's his name?"

"It was Mick Brady. He died last year."

"Oh, I'm sorry for your loss," Della said sincerely.

"Thank you," Cate said. "We have three kids—Aaron, Jilly, and Niko. Sounds like you are their aunt."

This was a lot to take in. "Wow," Della said.

"If you want, you could come to visit us. We live in wine country, California, in a town called Rosemary Run. We'd love to have you. We can talk through things and learn about each other," Cate offered.

Della cleared her throat, pushing back all of the emotions threatening to break her down. "That's very kind of you, Cate. It's a busy day for me today. Can I call you back another time?"

"Yeah, no pressure," Cate replied. "I just wanted to reach out and let you know we'd like to meet you. If Mick was still alive, I'm sure he would, too."

They exchanged contact information and hung up, Della feeling like she'd just been hit by a freight train.

Every emotion crashed over her like an overwhelming wave—excitement, confusion, and a twinge of sadness at the loss of the brother she had never known. She leaned against a wall, breathing deeply to regain her composure.

"Are you okay?" Malik asked. He must have sensed the change in her demeanor. "You look like you've just seen a ghost."

"Not a ghost, but something just as surprising," Della replied, her voice shaky as she processed the information. "I found out I have a brother, apparently. A biological brother."

"What?" Malik's brows shot up in disbelief. "That's incredible. Do you know anything about him?"

"That's what's overwhelming," Della admitted, running a

hand down the edges of her hair. "His name was Mick Brady. He died last year. I just talked to his sister, Cate, and she—she says I'm an aunt."

"She reached out to you?" Malik asked, his surprise softening into admiration for her unusual connection to the story. "You really never knew?"

"Yes, and no. My mother never told me much about my biological father, and I've never had any reason to think there was anyone else," Della said, frustration lacing her tone. "This is all shocking, to say the least. I don't know how to process it."

"Understandable," Malik said. "You'll figure it out. Isn't it time you leave here and get yourself dressed for the wedding? You don't want to show up looking like a fed there to make a bust, do you?"

"Right," Della replied, straightening. "Can I trust you to keep this under wraps … until I get it sorted?"

"You have my word," Malik promised.

"Thanks, Agent Washington," she said, grateful for his support. Della took a moment to refocus, casting aside the lingering emotions tied to the conversation with Cate. "Let's talk strategy for tonight's operation. Then I'll go get ready for the wedding."

Malik nodded. "No distractions. We focus on the kids. We recover as much as we can and put even more pressure on Sidewinder."

"I suppose it's pretty cut and dry, isn't it?"

"Textbook," he replied. "Not that things can't go wrong. They can. We know what we're doing, though."

"I hope we find Billy tonight," Della said. "My gut tells me he's still in town, but that he might not be for long."

Malik nodded. "Timing is everything. We've got our best team on this. If the boy is there, we will bring him home safely."

"Will I see you at the wedding?" Della asked.

"Yes, ma'am," Malik replied. "Agent Aziz, too. We wouldn't miss it."

Della smiled, then grabbed her bag and headed out the front doors of the station. Eric was there waiting for her, looking handsome in a sleek green SUV. He wasn't driving that earlier, which means he must have gone home for a clean suit and tie. Della wondered what he and Sylvia had talked about, or if they'd seen each other at all.

"Hey, there, pretty lady," Eric said as Della climbed into the passenger seat.

"Hi, Hami," she said. "Don't you look delicious?"

He glanced around quickly to see if anyone was watching, then leaned over and kissed her on the lips. "Delicious, huh? I'll take that as a compliment. Ready for a wedding?"

Something about the way he said the word wedding made them both think about more than just Laurel and Brad. Perhaps someday, Eric and Della would be marrying each other.

"It's hard to shift gears, but yes," Della replied. "You?"

"I feel like I'm supposed to say it's a bit odd to see an ex-girlfriend getting married, but it isn't, really," he said. "Laurel and Brad clearly belong together. And she wasn't the one for me. So, all's well that ends well. Right?"

Della nodded. "Right. Now take me back to the rental house so I can make myself presentable."

Della quickly changed into an elegant sleeveless midi dress with a twist at the waist. She touched up her hair and makeup, opting for her go-to—a sleek ponytail. She stashed her powder and lipstick into a coordinating clutch and slid on a pair of heels. It was fortunate that she'd packed the outfit, especially since she hadn't known there would be a wedding to attend. Something had told her to bring a nice dress, just in case. She was grateful for the intuition.

When she stepped out of the bathroom and into Eric's line of sight, his face lit up.

"Oh, D.," he said as he stood, "you're breathtakingly beautiful."

"Careful," she said with a smile. "You don't want to distract me and make us late for the wedding."

He raised his brows a few times. "Is that an invitation?"

"It's a promise for later. How's that?" she teased. "Now, be my hunky arm candy."

He laughed. "Says the real arm candy."

They locked up the house then climbed back into the SUV, excitement bubbling between them.

"Do you think we'll make it in time?" Della asked, glancing out the window as Eric drove and the scenery zipped by. The streets of Appleman's Gap were still littered with evidence of the storm's fury, though crews were working tirelessly to clear the debris.

"I hope so," Eric replied, his hands gripping the steering wheel tightly. "I wouldn't want to miss seeing Laurel and Brad get married. They deserve this moment."

"Yeah, they really do. It's like a beacon of hope amidst all this destruction." Della smiled to herself, her thoughts drifting to her friend and how happy she must feel right now. "Let's hope the weather cooperates."

The last remnants of storm clouds hung in the sky, but it

seemed like they were in the clear, at least for the moment. A few rays of sunlight broke through, casting a soft glow over the town.

Della shifted slightly in her seat, stealing a glance at Eric. She was grateful he was there, but the intensity of what was happening between them was still fresh in her mind. Not to mention, the news she'd received from Cate Brady had caught her off guard.

"You okay?" Eric asked suddenly, interrupting the silence. "You've gone quiet."

"Yeah, just thinking," she responded.

"I know." He glanced at her with concern. "It's a lot. But I'm proud of how we've handled everything. You've been so strong, and I know it's not easy."

She felt a warmth rush through her at his compliment. "Thanks, Hami. It helps to have you near. You've been strong, too, which is especially impressive because I know how worried sick you've been about Billy."

"Thank you. You're right. I have," he said. "It might be naive of me, but I feel like he's close by and that we're going to find him tonight."

They approached the Dane family estate, the once-familiar exterior now marred by scattered branches and bits of roofing material. Still, it stood intact. Della felt a swell of emotions at the sight. It was a refuge amidst the chaos.

"Ready for me to show you off?" Eric joked, flashing a grin as they parked.

"I'm ready."

Twenty-Six

"HOW'S IT GOING IN THERE?" Maggie asked through the bathroom door as Laurel put the finishing touches on her makeup. "Need anything?"

"Nope. I'm almost ready!" Laurel called back, adjusting her mascara and glancing in the mirror. She felt a flutter of nerves in her stomach, excitement mixing with anxiety as she mentally prepared for the ceremony ahead. After a whirlwind of a day, it was finally time to solidify her commitment to Brad in front of family and friends.

"Good. Hurry up. I think Ryan and Hazel are about to start a debate on whether or not this wedding is a good idea." Maggie teased from the other side of the door.

Laurel chuckled, imagining her siblings passionately discussing the merits of elopement versus full-blown, planned-out weddings. She knew how much they cared for her and wanted everything to be just right for the occasion, even amidst the uncertainty of the storm damages and the emotional fallout from the tornado. None of them knew what the destruction of the apple barn meant for the family business, but they'd have to figure something out before autumn arrived. It was their busiest time of year and the season when they made the majority of their income.

"I'll be out in a sec," Laurel replied, smoothing a stray hair back into place before dabbing a bit more lipstick onto her lips. Just as she finished, there was a soft knock on the door.

"Can I come in?" Brad asked, his voice low and teasing.

Laurel laughed softly. "You know you can't see me before the wedding."

"Please," he said dramatically, "everyone knows that's just superstition. I need to see you before I go insane out here."

"Hold on!" she called, looping a pearl bracelet Maureen had given her around her wrist. It was her something old. "Just a minute."

With one last check in the mirror to admire the sleek elegance of the gown and the way it hugged her growing belly, she took a deep breath, reminding herself that their love was about to be sealed with vows. That was what truly mattered. Who cared about silly superstitions?

"Okay, I'm ready," Laurel said finally as she swung the door open.

Brad stood on the other side, his expression shifting from anticipation to awe as he took in her radiant look. "Wow," he breathed, his eyes widening. "You look absolutely stunning." The sincerity in his voice made her feel special, cherished in a way that filled her heart with warmth.

"Thank you," she said, blushing slightly as she swirled around to give him a full view. "What do you think?"

"I think you'll have everyone in tears before the 'I do's' are said," he replied, stepping closer to wrap his arms around her waist. His touch sent a jolt through her, igniting all the emotions that had built up over the past months since they'd reunited here in Appleman's Gap. "Are you ready to get married?"

"More than ready," Laurel replied. "This is the next step in our journey together, and I can't wait to say 'I do.'"

"Good," he said, pulling back just enough to look her in the eye.

Laurel smiled, biting her lip as she stepped back. She turned to the door, "Let's not keep everyone waiting. I feel like they're all holding their breath out there."

Brad nodded, stepping back so that she could lead the way. "After you, my dazzling bride."

When they walked into the garden behind the house, Laurel felt her breath catch. It was everything she had imagined. The branches of the towering trees swayed gently in the breeze, the sun streaming down in golden rays as family and friends gathered around. Flowers decorated the space, their vibrant colors shining against the earth-toned backdrop of the house and the orchard behind it.

The soft sound of classical music drifted through the air, courtesy of Laurel's former bandmates, now seated on the grass, ready to play for the duration.

"You got them here!" she exclaimed, nodding at the brass quintet. "How, on such short notice?"

"I have my ways," Brad said sweetly. "Enjoy it."

Surrounded by loved ones—her siblings, parents, and close friends—she felt more alive than ever before.

"Look at them!" Laurel whispered to Brad, pointing at her family as they took their seats.

Her siblings were already laughing—no doubt sharing some inside joke—and her parents looked happy, which was a joy to see. Mack wasn't there, and Laurel was glad he'd decided to sit this one out. He was a nice enough man, seemingly, but there was still something strange about him. Laurel didn't want to think about it on her wedding day.

"Did Sarah make it?" she asked, scanning the crowd.

Brad shook his head. "I don't think so. Sorry, babe."

Laurel hadn't really expected her to be here, but she'd hoped.

"Just a few more moments until you're officially Mrs. Tate," Brad said, leaning in close to nip at her ear.

She shuddered, her heart racing at the thought. "Let's make this count."

At four o'clock sharp, Cornelius arrived at Laurel's side and extended his arm to walk her down the aisle. His gait was still a bit wobbly, but he'd been working so hard with his physical therapist over the past few months that you wouldn't notice anything wrong, if you didn't know to look for it. Laurel was overwhelmed with gratitude that her dad was alive and here for the special moment. It would have been heart wrenching to do it without him. He looked handsome in a suit and tie, his hair neatly combed.

"Ready, my darling daughter, apple of my eye?" Cornelius asked.

The phrase caught Laurel off guard and choked her up. She had completely forgotten, but Cornelius had called her the apple of his eye when she was a little girl. They had traipsed through the orchard together, laughing about how Laurel wasn't actually an apple. The term of endearment was incredibly meaningful, especially given the nature of their family business.

"Aww, I had forgotten about that, Dad," she said, reaching up to hug his neck. "I'm so glad you're here."

"Me, too. More than you know."

"Hey, did you ever hear if Jamie and the baby are safe?"

He smiled. "They're at her aunt's house, safe and sound. Nice of you to ask."

Laurel nodded. "And where are Lilly and Sully?" she asked.

Cornelius gestured toward one side of the garden where none other than Jimmy Paulson sat, holding both dogs on leashes. Jimmy waved enthusiastically when Laurel made eye contact.

"I didn't know Jimmy was coming. How great to have him here," Laurel said, a tear forming in her eye. "I can hardly believe how many people showed up for us even though this was last minute."

"I suppose that speaks to how highly they think of you and Brad," Cornelius said with a smile.

In a beautiful burst of sound, the brass quintet began to play Pachelbel's Canon in D. The tuba's long, low notes sung throughout the garden, followed by the French horn's smooth melody. Chillbumps covered Laurel's entire body and her baby moved gently in response to the music. The moment was pure perfection.

It was time.

They hadn't had a chance to rehearse their walk down the aisle, but somehow, Laurel and Cornelius were in perfect sync. They stepped in time to the beat, left feet first, as they moved closer to Brad, who was biting back tears as he stood tall and waited for his bride.

"Take good care of my baby girl," Cornelius said as he neared the altar and gave Laurel's hand to Brad.

"Yes, sir, Chief," Brad replied, then he and Laurel turned and climbed the steps in front of the officiant while Cornelius returned to his seat next to Maureen.

As they took their place beneath the floral arch, all Laurel could focus on was the warmth of Brad's hand in hers and the overwhelming love that surrounded them. The music flowed softly, and as she caught glimpses of her siblings and parents, they all had tears in their eyes, their expressions a blend of pride and joy.

"Dearly beloved," the officiant began, "we are gathered here today to celebrate the union of Laurel Dane and Brad Tate, joined together in love and commitment, to face life's challenges as one family."

Laurel took a deep breath, anchoring herself in this moment. She gazed into Brad's eyes, which were filled with unwavering support and affection. "Hello, wife," he whispered, his mouth barely moving, and she nodded, feeling a rush of emotions flood over her.

"Brad, do you take Laurel to be your lawfully wedded wife?" the officiant asked, and Brad's smile grew wider, his voice steady as he affirmed, "I do."

"And Laurel, do you take Brad to be your lawfully wedded husband?"

"I do," she replied.

"As you exchange your vows, may you find strength in one another, and may your love for each other grow deeper in each circumstance." The officiant looked between them, nodding for Brad to continue.

Brad cleared his throat, his eyes gleaming with sincerity. "Laurel, from the moment we met, you've brought light and laughter into my life. I promise to support you, encourage you, and walk beside you as we embark on this journey together. No matter what challenges come our way—whether they come from outside forces or within—I vow to be your partner and friend."

Tears streamed down Laurel's cheeks as she listened, heart swelling with gratitude for the man standing before her. "Brad," she began, "you have shown me what real love is. You've stood by me through every storm, both literally and metaphorically. I promise to cherish you, to stand with you through the good and the bad, and to grow together in love, forgiveness, and strength."

"Thank you for letting us join in this sacred moment," the officiant said, his voice warm and encouraging. "Let's now exchange rings as a token of your committed love."

The ceremony continued seamlessly, with Brad and Laurel slipping the rings onto each other's fingers. Brad had gotten them on short notice, too. Each ring shone brightly, symbolic of their commitment and love. A love that had flourished against the odds.

With the exchange of rings complete, the officiant beamed at them, ready to culminate this long-awaited moment. "By the power vested in me, I now pronounce you husband and wife. You may kiss the bride."

Brad wasted no time, pulling Laurel close as their lips met in a sweet kiss. Cheers erupted from the crowd. Joy and celebration washed over the gathering like the gentle spring breeze that rustled the leaves of the trees.

"This is it," Laurel whispered, breaking the kiss but holding on to Brad, their foreheads touching as they shared a private moment. Her face broke into a bright smile.

As friends and family stepped forward to congratulate them and shower them with love, it felt like the world had narrowed down to what mattered most. It was their moment.

"Look at you two!" Hazel exclaimed, wiping fake tears from her cheeks. "You're going to make me cry. Seriously though, this is the best thing I've seen in a long time. Y'all are sweet."

"You both look so happy!" Maggie chimed in, a big smile on her face as she snapped photos on her phone. "Let's get all the siblings in a picture before we lose the sunlight."

Ryan joined them, and they dove into an animated conversation about the highlights of the day. The atmosphere was a beautiful blend of laughter, tears, and sentimental moments. Even Cornelius and Maureen exchanged proud glances, the stress of the past year softened by love and hope for the future.

The party soon shifted toward another area of the back yard, where tables had been set up in the shade, adorned with flowers and decorations.

"Let's eat!" Brad announced, waving arms around.

"Husband, you did good," Laurel said. "I can hardly believe you pulled all this together. It hasn't even been twenty-four hours since we decided to pull the trigger. You're amazing."

He kissed her lightly on the lips, then placed a protective hand over their baby. "You're pretty amazing yourself, wife. You had a few short hours to doll yourself up, and here you are, looking like heaven. I'm the luckiest man in the world."

"Fate brought us together, and it brought us to this day," Laurel mused. "I'm grateful for every twist and turn that led us here."

Twenty-Seven

DELLA SMILED as she glided across the makeshift dance floor in Eric's arms. She didn't mind being seen with him, but she was holding back. It felt wrong to dance and have fun when Billy was out there somewhere.

"What's on your mind, D.?" Eric asked as he pulled her close.

She shrugged. "Billy, mostly."

She hadn't had a chance to tell Eric about the phone call from Cate Brady, let alone figure out how to properly navigate the ancestry website to verify Cate's claims for herself. Life seemed to be moving at warp speed.

"I know," he said. "It feels strange to do anything but be sad and worried. I don't think we should hold ourselves back, though. Life is a mix of ups and downs, highs and lows. We've taken every action we can to find Billy and bring him home. Hopefully, that will happen at the raid tonight. In the meantime, I think we should enjoy this moment."

"I guess you're right," Della said, relaxing into his arms. "It's complicated."

"It doesn't have to be."

"Do you think he'll like me?" she asked.

Eric pulled back to look her in the eye. "Billy?"

"Yeah. I mean, once he gets medical treatment and counseling and whatever else he needs after this ordeal. When we have time to get to know each other. Do you think he'll like me?"

"Of course, he will."

Della smiled a small smile, but she was skeptical. "I'm not sure I'm any good with kids, Hami. Maybe that's why God saw fit for me not to have my own."

At that, Eric stopped dancing and pulled Della into a tight embrace. "Stop. Don't go there," he said. "You're perfect and wonderful, exactly the way you are. I'm sorry if I ever made you feel any different."

Della fought sobs that threatened to spill out. There was a lot to unpack about her inability to have children. It was the most painful thing she'd experienced in life, thus far. It cut deep.

Just then, Jimmy appeared, dancing by himself and acting silly. He couldn't see Della's face and didn't realize he was walking into a private moment.

"Well, well, Agent Brady," he said playfully, "I see you're keeping close tabs on our person of interest. When I told you to stick with him, I didn't mean it quite this literally."

"Not a good time, Agent Paulson," Eric said sternly, wrapping an arm around Della and walking toward a quiet corner near the house.

"Oh," Jimmy said, following them. "Sorry about that. I didn't read the room."

Della chuckled softly, grateful for the brief distraction. "It's okay. Just some wedding nerves, I guess."

She was good at compartmentalizing and tucking her emotions away. Weren't all F.B.I. agents? It was part of their training.

Eric remained close, the concern in his eyes softening as he relaxed a little more. "I appreciate you keeping an eye out, though, Jimmy. It's a whirlwind today, and the last thing we need is for the media to cause any trouble at the wedding. I can't help but feel like those jackals are going to cause me trouble, sooner or later."

Jimmy nodded, shifting into a more serious demeanor. "Have any updates come through yet? We're keeping in touch with the teams assigned to the chapel raid."

Della exchanged glances with Eric, weighing the gravity of the situation against the joyful atmosphere surrounding them. "Not yet, but I trust they're doing everything they can. I hope we catch a break tonight."

"Same here," Eric said. "Laurel and Brad deserve this happiness without any more drama."

As they discussed logistics, Della continued to feel hopeful that they would find Billy. Afterward, everyone could settle back into life again, and she could address the new dynamics brought about by her unexpected familial ties.

After a while, Jimmy finally snorted and asked, "All right! Who wants to join me on the dance floor? I'm going back for round two."

"Count me in, buddy," Eric replied, breaking away from Della and throwing a playful punch at Jimmy's shoulder. "Let's show these people how to have a real party!"

Della couldn't help but laugh as the two men swept

toward the improvised dance area. She watched them, feeling a sense of belonging wrap around her heart. Perhaps she could indeed enjoy this moment without feeling guilty.

Drawing a deep breath, she stepped toward the dance floor as well, joining in the laughter and the music. She felt the heaviness in her chest lift slightly as she moved, reminded of the happiness in being with family and friends.

With each twirl, each laugh, and every moment spent dancing alongside Eric and Jimmy, she allowed herself to experience the magic of the occasion. The music swelled around her, encouraging her to let go of her doubts and worries, if only for a little while.

The atmosphere shifted as Laurel and Brad joined the dance floor, laughter spilling forth as they celebrated their newfound union. Seeing her friend so radiant and blissful centered Della. It reinforced the belief that happiness could flourish even in turbulent times.

"Look at those two!" Eric exclaimed, his eyes shining with admiration. "They truly make a beautiful couple."

Della nodded. "They do," she agreed. "It's inspiring to see them embrace love like this, especially after everything they've been through. I guess love wins, in the end."

As the beat pulsed through the air, the trio danced together—Della alongside Eric and Jimmy, falling into step as they moved to the rhythm of the music. Laughter filled the yard, and even though the concerns loomed overhead about Billy's safety, a sense of camaraderie enveloped them, pushing back against the worry.

Della caught a glimpse of Mikey, Maggie, Hazel, and Ryan dancing nearby, their faces alight with joy. It reminded her of how grateful she was to be friends with such a strong, supportive family, even one that felt a little fractured at moments. They represented hope, resilience, and the power of coming together in tough times.

She twirled, feeling the energy rise as the music shifted from a slow ballad to an upbeat tune, propelling everyone into an impromptu dance-off. "Are we really dancing now?" she laughed, her spirits lifting as they spun and grooved.

"Why not?" Jimmy shouted back, sweat already pooling along his brow. He pulled out a handkerchief and wiped his shiny, bald head. "We're here to celebrate. I didn't fly down from D.C. on short notice to sit around being bored. I do enough of that at work for the F.B.I. every day."

They all laughed together.

After a few more songs, Eric leaned in close to Della. "I'm glad we came," he said earnestly, his breath brushing against her hair. "This is amazing. I needed this more than I realized."

"Me too," Della replied.

Time passed quickly, and soon it was time for dinner to begin. The evening air cooled around them as they transitioned from one lively scene to another. Friends and family went to find their seats at the tables adorned with white tablecloths and floral arrangements. A celebratory feast awaited the newlyweds and their guests.

As they took their places, Della felt nostalgic. The warmth of the gathering filled her with a sense of belonging that felt so familiar, it was almost overwhelming. This was a community bound by love and resilience.

Had she become too isolated lately? Too focused on work? It was something she'd need to ponder.

Brad and Laurel were announced as Mr. and Mrs Tate, and cheers erupted around the tables. The couple burst into laughter, their happiness infectious as they beamed at one another.

"Welcome to the family, Brad!" someone shouted from the back, and the applause only grew louder.

Della felt her heart swell with happiness for her friend. "Aww," she said softly.

As the newlyweds moved to their seats at the head table, speechmaking and toasts began.

Mikey stood up first, raising his glass high, as Jess and their kids looked on proudly. "To the bride and groom! May your love be as strong as the apple trees that bloom in our backyard and as sweet as the cider Mom makes."

Cheers erupted again, and Laurel laughed, glancing at her parents, who were nodding with pride. The warmth enveloping the space felt like a shield against the uncertainties of the world outside. It didn't matter that the tornado had caused such devastating damage. The Danes and their loved ones and friends were happy to be alive, celebrating Laurel and Brad's special day.

Then it was Della's turn. She stood and cleared her throat, her eyes seeking Eric's as she raised her glass. "I want to toast to love. Love that we all experience in different ways, from friendship to family, and to new beginnings. To Laurel and Brad, may your love carry you through life's twists and turns. And may we all support each other in finding our own paths."

Applause accompanied her words, and Della took her seat again. She was part of something beautiful today, and it felt good.

Dinner was delicious Southern fare catered by Puckett's —fried chicken, collard greens, biscuits, and an assortment of desserts that made Della's mouth water. She was happy to indulge. Each bite tasted better than the last.

The merriment continued as Jimmy, Maggie, and Cornelius stood to toast the happy couple. By the time Cornelius was finished with his remarks, there wasn't a dry eye to be found. Everyone was so grateful that he was alive and well. It had been less than a year ago that they'd gathered at his funeral.

Life can turn on a dime.

Finally, as the event wound down and Laurel and Brad left for an impromptu honeymoon in the mountains, Della turned her attention to the raid scheduled to take place in a few hours. She gestured to Samira and Malik, letting them know.

"Are you heading to the station with us?" she asked Jimmy, her tone all business. "It's almost go-time."

"Absolutely," Jimmy replied, his energy shifting from the celebration back to the serious undertones of the investigation. "Let's coordinate with the teams. Maybe forensics got a hit on the car you found."

"Are we fully briefed on everyone's roles?" she asked, leading the charge out the door.

Jimmy nodded emphatically. "Yes, Agent Washington is overseeing logistics, while the tactical team preps for entry. We're in constant contact with the local units."

Della felt a rush of gratitude for her team. They worked well together, and everyone shared a common goal, which reminded her that they were more than colleagues. They were all in this fight together. "Good. Communication will be key."

"Finally," Eric said. "I'm so ready. I hope to be holding my son by the time the clock rolls over to tomorrow."

Twenty-Eight

"HERE WE GO," Della muttered to herself as they piled into Eric's SUV. She felt a reassuring presence as he sat beside her, his solid form a reminder that she was not alone. Malik and Samira followed in their own car.

The drive to the station was charged with anticipation. Della could feel the electricity in the air surrounding them, a heady mix of suspense and hope. They arrived, quickly stepping inside, and she could see the nerves reflected on the faces in the room.

"Okay, everyone, listen up!" Malik called out as the team gathered around a large table. "The intel we received about the chapel is solid. We're to move in as per the designated plan and make sure we keep communication open. A short time ago, we received results back from forensics. Billy Hampton's DNA was found in the car we recovered. If we're lucky, we're going to find him tonight and deliver him to the safety of Senator Hampton's arms. We have every reason to believe that the information Silas Aguilar, AKA Sidewinder, gave us is accurate. He's in protective custody and afraid for his life. Making a deal with us was his best chance of survival."

Della nodded, her eyes scanning the faces of her colleagues. "Tonight is about saving Billy. We have to act decisively and with care. No slip-ups."

A few heads bobbed in agreement.

"Right," Jimmy added, his voice steady. He'd been keeping close tabs on the investigation from D.C. and was fully briefed and eager to assist. "We'll go in as quietly as possible, securing the perimeter before making our way inside. Surveillance cameras have already been disabled, but we still need to be cautious. Our biggest concern is The Cradler's backup. He won't want to let anyone go without a fight."

The team shared knowing glances, steeling themselves against the severity of what lay ahead. Della felt a pulse of adrenaline surge through her as the plan unfolded, each step clicking into place like the gears of a well-oiled machine.

"Before we move out, I want to remind everyone to trust your gut," Della said, looking each one of them in the eye. "If something feels off, you pull out. This is about protecting our lives and the life of that little boy."

The room murmured in agreement, and Della could feel the resolve building among them.

As the team prepared and there was a quiet moment, Erik turned to Della. "Stay close to me tonight, D. I want to make sure you're safe."

Della nodded. "As close as I can."

"Good."

The air hummed with anticipation as they exited the station and loaded into their vehicles. In the distance, the outline of the chapel broke through the skyline. It was brazen for The Cradler to hold Billy so close to the police station. Perhaps he was looking for attention, more than anything else.

As they arrived on-site, Della's instincts kicked into high gear. The adrenaline coursed through her veins, sharpening her focus. She put her game face on, aligning herself with the mission's objectives.

"All right, let's move," Malik directed, his voice steady but quietly intense. "Stay alert, keep your eyes peeled."

The group made its way discreetly through the under-brush surrounding the chapel, approaching the entrance cautiously, with Malik leading the way. They could hear faint sounds of voices filtering through the walls—a mix of laughter and threats echoed from within.

Malik signaled for everyone to halt as they arrived at the edge of the property, just out of sight of the chapel's entrance. The air felt thick with tension, each agent's shaky breath a steady reminder of the stakes at hand.

"Remember, the safety of the kid is paramount," Malik whispered, his eyes narrowing as he surveyed the area. "We don't know how many people are inside or if they're armed."

Della nodded, adjusting the strap of her gear and mentally preparing herself.

Just then, Jimmy, who had positioned himself with the surveillance team behind the chapel, whispered over the radio, "I see two guards near the entrance. They're distracted, but we need to move quick before they realize something's off."

"Copy that," Malik responded, gesturing for everyone to fall into position.

Della felt her stomach twist into knots as she readied

herself for what was about to unfold. This was their moment to shine. It was the culmination of many hours spent gathering intel, chasing leads, and facing the fear of the unknown —not just since Billy had been taken, but ever since The Cradler's deranged father had begun terrorizing this town.

"On my mark," Malik instructed, as the agents huddled close.

"Three ... two ... one ... go!" Malik shouted, and the team sprang into action, moving swiftly toward the entrance of the chapel.

They approached with stealth, quickly neutralizing the guards lurking outside. Della's heart raced as they worked in unison, slipping through the doorway with fluidity born from practice and instinct. The chapel's interior was dimly lit, cast with shadows that twisted unnaturally against the walls.

"Clear!" she called out, leading the way as they moved cautiously through the entrance.

Inside, disarray spun around them. Folding chairs stood askew, decorations lay scattered, and remnants of an unfocused event littered the ground. Della's mind raced as she took in the surroundings, searching for signs of life, especially that of a young boy.

"Where are they?" Malik whispered urgently as they moved cautiously down the main aisle of the chapel, weapons at the ready.

Della glanced around, her senses heightened. "Let's split up and check the rooms," she suggested. "We need to cover ground quickly."

"I'll take the left side," Malik said, heading toward the adjoining rooms. "Aziz and I will sweep through the back. You and the rest of the team take the right."

Della nodded. As she ventured down the corridor on the right, tension crackled in the air. Each door they passed was a portal into uncertainty. Sensing their time was limited, Della steeled herself and reached for the first door, pushing it open slowly. It creaked eerily, echoing in the silence.

The room was empty, furnished only with folding chairs and a table laden with old tattered ritual books. "Nothing here," she said, glancing quickly over her shoulder before moving to the next door, which also yielded no results.

"Keep moving. We have to find him," she said.

They continued their search, hastily checking each room. It was a race against time as they methodically moved deeper into the chapel. With each empty room, Della's heart sank a little more. The fear of failure gnawed at the edges of her resolve.

"Over here!" Malik shouted suddenly, breaking through the eerie stillness.

Della rushed to his side as he finished opening a door at the end of the hallway, his expression leaning towards cautious hope.

"Please let this be it," she whispered as she peered into the small, dimly lit room.

Inside, they found a makeshift sleeping area, complete with a tattered blanket thrown haphazardly over an old cot. The air was thick with the musty scent of abandonment, but it was the sight of something else that made Della's heart race. A small child's shoes, scuffed and worn out, sat near the cot.

"Billy," Della murmured, her voice choked with emotion. "He has to be nearby."

Just then, the sudden sound of voices flooded the hallway.

Diverse shouts and muffled laughter echoed, sending chills down Della's spine. They weren't alone.

"That sounded just outside the chapel," Malik said.

"Yeah, and it sounded too close for comfort," Della added, her heart pounding as the fear of discovery loomed. "We need to find Billy, and fast."

They moved back into the corridor, scanning the area for anything that could lead them to him. The chatter outside seemed to increase, growing louder and rowdier.

"Let's check the next room," Della suggested, gesturing for Malik to follow her once again.

They approached the door at the end of the corridor cautiously, readying themselves for whatever they might find beyond it. Della took a deep breath and pressed her ear against the door, listening intently. The sound of laughter continued, mingled with what appeared to be a faint voice. Was that a child?

"Open it!" Malik urged, his voice barely above a whisper.

Della nodded, her pulse racing as she slowly turned the handle, pushing the door open just enough to peek inside.

Inside the room, illuminated by a single overhead light, was a small group of men gathered around a makeshift table, playing cards while exchanging raucous laughter. To Della's horror, in the corner of the room sat a young boy, visibly frightened, his wide eyes darting over to the door whenever it creaked.

"Billy!" Della gasped softly, her heart racing. Without thinking, she stepped into the room and raised her weapon, making her presence known. "F.B.I.! Get your hands up!"

Malik burst in right behind her, ready to back her. The

laughter of the men immediately ceased, confusion flooding their faces as they realized who had entered.

"What the hell?" one of the men exclaimed, dropping their cards in shock as he leaped up from his seat.

"Billy, come here!" Della called out, extending her hand toward the frightened boy.

"Stay back!" one of the men shouted, brandishing a knife as he positioned himself in front of the child.

"You need to let him go. He's just a child!" she said.

The intruder's hardened expression told her he wasn't ready to back down.

"Stay where you are, or he gets it!" the man snarled, brandishing the weapon toward Billy, who shrank back against the wall.

The poor kid was terrified.

"Drop the knife and nobody gets hurt," Malik warned, stepping in front of Della, ready to protect her and the child if things escalated. "You're outnumbered, and it's over for you."

The other men in the room exchanged glances, weighing their odds. They hadn't expected any interruptions, let alone armed federal agents.

"Shut it!" the knife-wielding man shouted.

"Please!" Billy whimpered, his small frame shaking.

"Billy, stay back!" Della called, her heart breaking for the fear in his voice. "We're here to help you. Trust me. I'm a friend of your dad's."

Suddenly, the sound of sirens wailed outside, and Della knew that reinforcements had arrived. The realization seemed to snap the man back into focus, fury dancing in his eyes. "You brought them here, didn't you?"

All her instincts screamed for action. "Malik, cover me!" she shouted as she lunged forward with determination, moving as quickly as she could.

Before the man could react, she positioned herself between him and Billy, arms raised. "You don't have to do this."

"Get away from him!" he spat, the knife shaking in his grip.

"Please!" Billy cried again, his little hands clenched into fists at his sides. "I just want to go home."

"I'm not going to let anything happen to you, I promise," Della reassured him.

An opportunity arose when one of the other men, seemingly spooked by the swiftness of the situation, took a step back, creating an avenue. Della didn't hesitate.

"Now!" she urged, lunging forward as Malik followed her lead.

"Drop it!" Malik shouted, drawing his weapon and aiming it at the man with the knife.

In that split-second distraction, Della seized the moment. She lunged forward, tackling the man to the ground, forcing his arm with the knife away from Billy. The clatter of the weapon hitting the floor echoed in the small room.

"Billy! Get out of here!" she yelled as she wrestled with the man beneath her.

The young boy didn't need to be told twice. He scrambled to his feet and darted toward the door, where Samira stood poised, ready to intercept.

"Come on, buddy. You're safe now," Samira urged, quickly ushering Billy out of harm's way.

The man Della wrestled with roared in frustration and

desperation, attempting to break free. She could feel the panic emanating from him as he struggled against her.

"Stop moving!" Della warned, drawing on all her training.

She managed to pin his wrist against the floor and reached for her handcuffs. Just as she clicked them over his wrist, the door burst open, and two more agents rushed in.

"What's the status?" one of them shouted, immediately sizing up the situation.

"We've got this under control," Malik said, still trying to keep an eye on Billy as he moved cautiously toward the exit.

Della secured the cuffs around the man and rolled him onto his back. He glared up at her, panting, and she could see the realization hit him. He wasn't getting out of this mess.

"More backup is on the way," one of the other agents said, keeping watch at the entrance. "Is the child okay?"

Della stood, still watching the first man carefully. "He's safe. We got him," she confirmed.

Relief washed over her as she took a moment to catch her breath.

"Where are the other perps?" Malik asked.

"No idea," Della said, her voice steady but laced with worry. "They might have fled when they heard the sirens."

"Let the team search the rest of the chapel," Malik urged, glancing toward the door where Billy had exited. "You go and be with the Senator and his son. Good work, Agent Brady."

A tear formed in Della's eye. "You sure are coming into your own, Agent Washington. If I didn't know better, I'd think you were a senior agent who'd been doing this for many years. Good work to you, too."

Della took a quick glance around the room, ensuring

things were settling down, then she went outside to find one of the most beautiful sights she'd laid eyes on in her entire life. There, Eric knelt on the damp grass, Billy's little arms wrapped tightly around his neck.

The scene struck a chord deep within her, a surge of emotion overwhelming her as she watched the man she loved cradle his son. Billy's small frame quaked against his father, clinging to him for dear life. The raw vulnerability in their embrace made her tear up, yet a smile crept across her face.

"He's safe, Hami," she said. "We did it. The Cradler is still out there, but tonight is a victory. We brought your sweet boy home."

TO BE CONTINUED.

Get Book 4 in the series, *Those Who Chase Her*.

* * *

Join Kelly's mailing list for updates and bonus content,
including your free Kelly Utt short story!

Enjoy this book?

A note from Author Kelly Utt

Did you enjoy this book? You can make a big difference.

Honest reviews of my books help bring them to the attention of other readers.

If you've enjoyed this book, I would be very grateful if you could spend just five minutes leaving a review (it can be as short as you like) on the book's retail page where you purchased and on Goodreads or BookBub.

Thank you very much.

STANDARDS OF STARLIGHT BOOKS
KELLY UTT

Kelly Utt writes emotional, pulse-pounding suspense, family saga, and women's fiction novels. The stakes are high. The twists and turns will keep you on the edge of your seat.

Kelly was raised by a dad who would read a book, ask her to read it, too, and then insist they discuss it together, igniting her passion for life's big questions. That passion is often reflected in her novels, giving them a depth which leaves readers wanting more and thinking about her stories long after the last lines are read.

Kelly holds a Bachelor's degree in psychology from the University of Tennessee, Knoxville and a master's degree in interactive media and communications from Quinnipiac University.

She lives in Nashville, Tennessee with her husband and sons. She also writes novels with one of her sons as the combined pen name Christopher Kelly.

www.kellyutt.com

www.ingramcontent.com/pod-product-compliance
Lightning Source LLC
Chambersburg PA
CBHW061803190726
48289CB00007B/2046